RACE FOR THE CURE
A TIME / SPACE ADVENTURE

ED Sims

Contents

Prologue 1
Pandemics

Excerpts from The History Channel

www.history.com/news/pandemics

As civilizations flourished, so did infectious diseases. A large number of people living in close proximity to each other and to animals, often with poor sanitation and nutrition, provided fertile breeding grounds for disease. And new overseas trading routes spread the infections far and wide, creating the first global pandemic.

Three of the deadliest pandemics in recorded history were caused by a single bacterium, *Yersinia pestis*, a fatal infection otherwise known as the plague. The Plague of Justinian arrived in Constantinople, the capital of the Byzantine Empire, in 541 CE. Plague-ridden fleas on black rats feeding on grain that came as tribute to Emperor Justinian from conquered Egypt carried the plague across the Mediterranean Sea from Egypt. It decimated Constantinople and spread like wildfire across Europe, Asia, North Africa, and Arabia, killing an estimated 30 to 50 million people, possibly half of the world's population.

"People had no real understanding of how to fight the plague other than trying to avoid sick people," says Thomas Mockaitis, a history professor at DePaul University. "As to how the plague ended, the best guess is that the majority of people in a pandemic somehow survive, and those who survive have immunity."

The plague never really went away, and when it returned 800 years later, it killed with reckless abandon. The Black Death, which hit Europe in 1347, claimed an astonishing 200 million lives in just four years. As for how to stop the disease, people still had no scientific understanding of contagion, says Mockaitis, but they knew that it had something to do with proximity. That's why forward-thinking officials in the Venetian-controlled port city of Ragusa decided to keep newly arrived sailors in isolation until they could prove they weren't sick. At first, sailors were held on their ships for 30 days. As time went on, they increased the forced isolation to 40 days, a quarantine—the origin of the word "quarantine" and the start of its practice in the Western world.

"That definitely had an effect," says Mockaitis. London never really caught a break after the Black Death. Named the Great Plague of London, it resurfaced roughly every 10 years from 1348 to 1665—40 outbreaks in just over 300 years. And with each new plague epidemic, 20 percent of the men, women, and children living in the British capital were killed.

By the early 1500s, England imposed the first laws to separate and isolate the sick. Homes stricken by plague were marked with a bale of hay strung to a pole outside. If they had infected family members, they had to carry a white pole when they went out in public. Cats and dogs were believed to carry the disease, so there was a wholesale massacre of hundreds of thousands of animals. The Great Plague of 1665 was the last and one of the worst of the centuries-long outbreaks, killing 100,000 Londoners in just seven months. All public entertainment was banned, and victims were forcibly shut into their homes to prevent the spread of the disease. Red crosses were painted on their doors along with a plea for forgiveness: "Lord have mercy upon us." As cruel as it was to shut up the sick in their homes and bury the dead in mass graves, it may have been the only way to bring the last great plague outbreak to an end.

Smallpox was endemic to Europe, Asia, and Arabia for centuries, killing three out of ten people it infected and leaving the rest with pockmarked scars. But the death rate in the Old World paled in comparison to the devastation wrought on native populations in the New World when the smallpox virus arrived in the 15th century with the first European explorers. The indigenous peoples of modern-day Mexico and the United States had zero natural immunity to smallpox, and the virus cut them down by the tens of millions. "There hasn't been a kill-off in human history to match what happened in the Americas—90 to 95 percent of the indigenous population wiped out over a century," says Mockaitis. "Mexico's population went from 11 million people pre-conquest to one million post-conquest."

Centuries later, smallpox became the first virus epidemic to be ended by a vaccine. In the late 18th century, a British doctor named Edward Jenner discovered that milkmaids infected with a milder virus called cowpox seemed immune to smallpox. Jenner famously inoculated his gardener's 9-year-old son with cowpox and then exposed him to the smallpox virus with no ill effect. "The annihilation of smallpox, the most dreadful scourge of the human species, must be the final result of this practice," wrote Jenner in 1801. And he was right. It took nearly two more centuries, but in 1980 the World Health Organization announced that smallpox had been completely eradicated from the face of the Earth.

Infectious diseases have been with mankind for as long as recorded history. They are disorders caused by organisms, many of which live in and on our bodies—such as bacteria, viruses, fungi, or parasites—and are normally harmless or even helpful. They are with us just as much as the air we breathe.

However, under certain conditions, some organisms may cause disease. Despite all the advances made in medical science, microbiologists are still unable to foresee the onset of an infectious disease epidemic reliably. Mankind is at the mercy of diseases for which cures have not yet been discovered or until they are.

Prologue 2

Brazil

1822-1824

For the past two years, Nicolas da Silva had fought tirelessly for his country's independence. The war had stretched from February 1822, when the first skirmishes ignited, until March 1824, when the Portuguese garrison in Montevideo surrendered. It had been a bloody and arduous conflict, but Brazil had finally secured its independence from the United Kingdom of Portugal. On December 1, 1824, the emperor of the newly independent Brazilian Empire was crowned, a symbol of the hard-fought victory.

Now that the war was over, Nicolas sat alone outside the garrison. The adrenaline and focus that had sustained him during battle were gone, replaced by the quiet emptiness of peacetime. As he contemplated the few meager possessions he had to begin his new life with, it all felt surreal: his mustering-out pay of 24 reis, his worn soldier's uniform, sword, rifle, sidearm, and canteen. His belongings were limited to an army blanket, a saddle, and saddlebags containing minimal provisions and ammunition. His one true companion on this journey back to civilian life was Balduin, his sturdy horse, whom he had named "brave friend" in honor of the bond they had formed during the war. As he stroked the horse's mane, he couldn't help but wonder what the future held for him.

His thoughts inevitably turned to his home in Rio Verde, a place that had seemed like a distant memory during the war.

It had been years since he'd seen his family or the familiar rolling hills of the region. The command he had been attached to had steadily moved south, chasing down Portuguese forces until the decisive final battle brought them to the garrison, where he now found himself. Rio Verde was nearly 2,500 kilometers away—a daunting distance. He was nearly as far from home as he could possibly be in this vast land.

Yet, despite the distance, the journey itself did not worry Nicolas. He could follow the Paraná River almost the entire length of his trip. The river, with its winding paths and nourishing waters, would provide food and drink for both him and Balduin. The route was well-worn, trodden by travelers and soldiers for centuries. Time, however, would be his true challenge. He estimated it would take just over two months to complete the trek, assuming he encountered no major setbacks. But with the war behind him and no pressing matters to delay him, Nicolas felt a flicker of hope. This was his chance to start anew. And with nothing to tie him down, he set out on his journey northward with determination.

Three days into his journey, as he neared the small village of Mercedes, something unexpected happened. A sudden wave of nausea and weakness overtook him. He had endured the harshest conditions of war—scarcity, injury, exhaustion—but this was different. His body felt hollow, as though drained of strength. At first, he thought it might be due to a lack of proper nourishment or hydration. After all, he had been living on rations for months. Hoping to restore his energy, he sought refuge in a local tavern.

Upon entering the dimly lit establishment, Nicolas noticed the uneasy glances from the other patrons. It was as though his very presence stirred a deep suspicion in them. He shrugged it off, paid for a meal, and sat down to eat, though it was hard to ignore the distance the others kept from him. His funds were meager, but they were enough to buy him ample portions of fish, bread, and ale. Still, he couldn't shake the feeling that something was wrong. The tavern was quiet, and the tension in the air was palpable.

When his meal was served, Nicolas finally asked the tavern keeper why everyone seemed to be avoiding him. The answer sent a chill down his spine. "You are the fourth soldier to pass through here after the war," the tavern keeper explained, his voice heavy with foreboding. "Each of the others appeared just as you do—pale, weak, unable to eat without retching. Since their passing through, nearly a quarter of our people have fallen ill with a sickness that devours them from the inside. Many of us have lost family members and friends. We fear you may be bringing the same illness with you."

Nicolas felt his stomach twist with fear. Could it be true? Was this weakness he felt not just exhaustion but something far worse? He had been through hell during the war, but nothing had left him this weak or nauseated. The fear gnawed at him as he continued eating, his body rebelling against every bite. A sudden and overwhelming urge to defecate and vomit hit him like a hammer, and he rushed outside. He barely made it to the tavern's steps before collapsing in a violent fit of vomiting and diarrhea, leaving him slumped in his own filth.

In that moment, as he lay on the cold, hard ground, Nicolas knew he was gravely ill. He lacked the strength to stand, let alone continue his journey. The people of Mercedes, terrified of contagion, made a decision. Though cruel, they believed it was for their safety. They dragged Nicolas' limp body to the edge of the village, abandoning him beneath a large oak tree. They promised to return with provisions, but it wasn't until the second day that a few dared approach him again. By then, it was too late. What they found was beyond horrific—Nicolas had been reduced to little more than a husk, his body emptied of all life. His closest companions would not have recognized him.

Within a week, the entire village of Mercedes succumbed to the illness. Within two weeks, every resident was dead. Within a month, a quarter of Brazil's population had contracted what would come to be known as *The Mercedes Virus*. And soon, it became a pandemic that ravaged the world.

Like the Great Plague of London, which had resurfaced time and again over centuries, *The Mercedes Virus* returned 120 years later in 1948 and again in 2040, each time spreading devastation in its wake.

Chapter 1
May 30, 2042

The two-engine airplane landed at the Meko Ryuk Airport on Nunivak Island, Alaska, with only one passenger aboard. Dr. Amaqjuaq Kannak landed with only his lightly packed backpack strapped casually across one shoulder. Because he knew his mission in advance, he knew he wouldn't remain long on the Island. Amaq, as his non-Inuit friends called him, had spent the last two years studying a virus that had viciously attacked the entire world; its newest pandemic was first identified in 2040 by Dr. Alexander Rhondo as a virus that had identical symptoms as the Mercedes Virus of the early 19th century and again in 1948.

That same year, in 2040, Amaq received his Doctorate at Beijerinck Institute of Medical Science in Minneapolis, Minnesota, where he studied Virology, a branch of microbiology that deals with the study of viruses. Having been given a grant to study the new Mercedes Virus at the Institute's laboratories, he had remained in Minneapolis, somewhat happily, somewhat not so happy. Happy because being raised by his tribe in northern Alaska, he was still in the northern climes and had not received a commission somewhere in one of the hotter southern states. Unhappy because he had not been home since he graduated from high school ten years ago in Utqiagvik, also known as Barrow, Alaska, the northernmost city in the United States, and home to the Iñupiat, an indigenous Inuit ethnic group, for more than 1,500 years.

Unlike the few classmates who went on to college at Iḷisaġvik College in his hometown, which was founded primarily to provide an education based on the Inupiaq cultural heritage to the residents of the North Slope Borough, Amaq chose to attend the University of Alaska in Fairbanks to study biological sciences, working construction jobs in the summer months to meet the costs. But instead of returning home to serve his community after earning his BS degree, he went on to study for his Doctorate at Beijerinck Institute of Medical Science.

"Welcome to Nunivak Island Dr. Kannak," he heard a young woman say as he stepped off the airplane. Amaq returned the greeting and followed her to a car and its driver, who had awaited his arrival. Sitting in the back seat with Amaq, the woman introduced herself: "I'm Dr. Amanda Kane. I'll be working very closely with you while you're here at Braxton. Our project will require the coordinated efforts of both a physicist with a background in quantum physics as well as the *Time/Space Project* and a microbiologist with a background in virology. I've been working with the Federal Bureau of Scientific Advancement (FBSA) since its early experiments with time/space travel nearly nine years ago."

Making a quick assessment of his new acquaintance, Amaq questioned the timeline he estimated, that if it took the usual eight years to receive her Doctorate and nine years working as a physicist with FBSA, she must be at least thirty-five years old. Yet, everything about her suggested a much younger woman. He would have pictured a thirty-five-year-old physicist to be anything from what he observed. She was shapely, soft-spoken, wore her brown hair loosely around her shoulders, and had very pleasing soft facial features, not what he would define as beautiful, but very pretty and pleasing to the eye.

"Only having been briefed, the emphasis on 'brief,'" Amaq replied, "I'm only vaguely knowledgeable about the *Time/Space Project*, so I welcome access to any resource that will further prepare me for my mission. I had no idea. However, I would be working with such a notable and lovely, I might add, physicist. I've read only a sampling of your work. But it's the evaluation of your peers that appeared in a 'Science Tomorrow' report that impressed me. I'm elated that I'll be working with such an esteemed physicist."

"And it's with great admiration of your work that I'm equally grateful that we'll be working together," Dr. Kane responded.

At that, they both looked at each other, the beginning of a smile appearing on both, which emerged into outward expressions of laughter. "Well," Dr. Kane offered. "Now that we've exchanged the perfunctory niceties and agree to both being members of the mutual admiration society, what do you say we head to the cafeteria when we get to Braxton and get better acquainted? We're almost there."

After traveling 4½ miles or so southwest of the airport, they arrived at the entrance of a rather nondescript four-story gray building with a sign identifying it as:

BRAXTON RESEARCH LABORATORIES

The Federal Bureau of Scientific Research

NUNIVAK ISLAND, ALASKA, USA

After making their selections from the cafeteria line, to be undisturbed, they chose a booth in a far corner. Dr. Kane opened the conversation, "I suspect, Dr. Kannak, that you're quite happy to be visiting your homeland. I find it fascinating that one, you are one hundred percent Inupiaq, and Utqiagvik has been home to your indigenous tribe for more than fifteen hundred years; two, that from that unlikely background you have risen to become one of the nation's foremost authorities on viruses; and three, how coincidental it is that a facility, whose proximity was built so close to your home, would be mankind's last hope of overcoming a virus that, if left unchecked, could probably decimate the world of human existence."

"Please address me as Amaq, the shortened name that my friends call me," Amaq replied. "It hadn't been my intention to allow myself to so completely estrange my hometown and my people. But that is in fact what happened. So, I do hope that I'll be able to spend some time visiting my hometown and my family in Utqiagvik. It's only about 1800 miles northeast from here. And since there is no guarantee that our project will succeed, I'd like to make that visit prior to launching our project even if it's for only a short time."

Perhaps because he'd asked her to address him by his first name, Dr. Kane noticed the man, not the doctor, for the first time. Replacing the professional title of Doctor with his given name somehow made their association more personable.

Since he spoke with a learned command of the English language as well as social graces, he was far from what one would expect, considering his early beginnings in an indigenous tribal community. Although he wasn't especially tall, his erect stance, broad shoulders and slim waist gave the appearance that he was. His skin was naturally dark, but it could have passed for a healthy sun tan. He was clean shaven and his black shiny hair was close- cropped. His facial features were a definite clue as to his ancestry, with a high forehead, dark brown slightly oblique eyes with heavy black eye brows. In all, he was quite handsome.

Dr. Kane continued the conversation, "Thank you for that token of friendship. I would like it very much if you called me Amanda. But concerning your visit home, I'm quite sure that the gravity of our mission is such that time is of the very essence and you will probably have to wait until you return before you can visit your family, if then. I'm sorry."

"I understand," Amaq said. "I should have expected that to be the case. I know of no one whose life hasn't been affected by the Mercedes Virus. And being as close to it as I've been, I'm thankful that I haven't been infected. Nor has any member of my family. Nor anybody else in Utqiagvik. But, like everyone else, I've had to put my personal life on hold and will continue to do so until a vaccine is finally produced. I'll phone my parents later this evening. They, too, will understand."

Needless to say, all scientists and medical professionals, especially microbiologists, had put more than their personal lives on hold, working endless hours and usually eating meals prepared for them at their workplaces and even sleeping on cots at their workplaces.

For them, they were the generals in germ warfare against all humanity, a war in which the victims suffered greatly with general flu symptoms, but attacking and killing all living cells, the virus was compounded severely by muscular degeneration, or to be more descriptive, the shriveling up of muscles causing unimaginable pain, including throat muscles, causing eventual inability to swallow; and the shriveling up of all internal organs. Starvation and dehydration quickly follow. The last organ to be attacked before death was the brain. People painfully degenerated literally into nothing left but putrid skin and rotting bones. As yet, there had been no survivors. Since it had claimed its first victim in 2040, the Mercedes Virus pandemic has killed 42 million people worldwide in two years.

"When is my indoctrination scheduled to begin?" Amaq asked.

"As soon as we finish lunch," Amanda replied. "The team is meeting in the conference room as we speak."

Chapter 2
1948

Six physicists were seated around the spacious conference room, each a specialist overseeing a segment of the *Time/Space Project.*

"Welcome to Braxton, Dr. Kannak. We've anxiously been awaiting your arrival. My name is Dr. Kenneth Willard, the Project Director. I see you've already met Dr. Kane. You will get to know the other physicists seated here as they present their portion of this meeting.

"As you already know," he continued, "we here at Braxton have, over the past nine years, successfully developed a machine we call the Transporter, that can transport matter into the future or the past... a time machine if you will... and a small device similar to your everyday TV remote control that can communicate with home base here in Braxton to activate the reverse process and return the time traveler to home base. We have named the project the *Time/Space Project...* that is: projecting matter through time and space.

"Also, as you know, your function as a virologist will be to be transported back in time to retrieve a sample of a microbe that's required to develop a vaccine that will provide immunity to the Mercedes Virus."

"Thank you, Dr. Willard," Amaq replied. "I'm looking forward to meeting all of you and working with you. And, yes, I did discover a microbe that is required to develop a vaccine for the virus that's plaguing humanity, but not in the usual way. For months, I searched unsuccessfully for a cure... a test-tube search using time-proven scientific methods in the laboratory. Then, in my research of the Mercedes Virus of 1948, for the hundredth time it seemed, I discovered something I'd previously missed: a microbe that was used to deactivate an enzyme that was required for the virus to spread, not only in one's body, but from one person to another. It was the removal of that enzyme that eventually saved the lives of millions of people. And it's that same microbe that scientists need to deactivate the enzyme in today's Mercedes Virus, a process aptly called *enzyme deactivation*.

"That microbe is named Fusarium circinatum, a fungal plant pathogen whose most common host is the Monterey pine, a tree which was native to the Central Coast of California and Mexico (Guadalupe Island and Cedros Island), but became extinct in the late twentieth century. And along with the extinction of the Monterey pine, Fusarium eventually died out too some years later."

"So, what's your game plan to retrieve this fungal plant pathogen?" another one of the scientists asked.

"From home base here in Braxton," Amaq answered. "Dr. Kane and I are to travel back in time and space, get a sample of Fusarium, and then travel back to home base with a sample in tow. The game plan is simple. But the game... maybe not so much. You see, we first have to find a sample. And that may not be so easy."

The first presenter rose and said, "Again, welcome to the exciting island of Nunivak, Dr. Kannak, where 24 hours of daylight in the summer keeps us groggy from lack of sleep, and

24 hours of darkness in the winter keeps us in the dark about everything." Everyone chuckled. "I'm Dr. Oliver Birmingham. I oversee the mathematical applications of the project. And I won't even try to explain how, over the past nine years, we finally established a mathematical theory that was conclusive, if you promise not to try to explain your theory of enzyme deactivation. However, I would like for you to explain to us just how it is going to slow, or even eventually eradicate the Mercedes Virus."

"Certainly," Amaq replied. "First, understand that the Mercedes Virus we're at war with today is identical to the Mercedes Virus of 1948, when scientists finally were able to eradicate it in 1952 with a vaccine they finally developed successfully. So, all we really had to do was duplicate the vaccine serum they had developed. Which we did... or thought we did… but it didn't work. We were scientifically justified in thinking that the virus had either changed or had become resistant to the serum. It was my accidental discovery that with Fusarium. They had deactivated an enzyme that was a catalyst for its growth. When that is introduced to the serum we've already developed, we are certain it will arrest the growth and the spread of the virus just as it did in 1952. The only problem there, however, is that Fusarium became extinct around 1980. And that's where our paths meet. The *Time/Space Project* gives us the means to go back in time prior to 1980 to retrieve a sample of that fungal plant."

"How can just one sample provide enough microbes to make enough serum to inoculate everyone with the vaccine?" another scientist asked.

"Knowing that only about a million microbes can be extracted from one plant, it doesn't stand to reason that it will go nearly far enough to make enough serum for a global inoculation program. But remember, these microbes live in a fungal plant, or mushroom, if you will. And under the right conditions, with the new facility we are building to grow the mushrooms that mature rapidly and multiply exponentially, we calculate that within one year they will provide for enough serum to globally arrest the spread of the virus.

"If there are no more questions," Dr. Willard said, "I suggest we proceed with the meeting to familiarize our new friend with the *Time/Space Project*. Dr. Emmit, would you please explain Time/Space for Dr. Kannak?"

"Certainly," Dr. Emmit replied. "According to the theory of special relativity," he explained, "time slows down or speeds up depending on how fast an object moves. And according to the theory of general relativity[1] gravity can bend time. Picture a four-dimensional fabric called Time/Space. When anything that has mass sits in the middle of that piece of fabric, gravity causes it to dimple the fabric or bend Time/Space. The bending of Time/Space causes objects to move on a curvature of space we know as gravity[2]. Both theories have been proven with GPS satellite technology.

---

[1] Tillman, N. T., Dutfield, S., & Bartels, M. (2024, October 29). *What is the theory of general relativity? Understanding Einstein's space-time revolution.* Space.com. https://www.space.com/17661-theory-general-relativity.html
[2] Mann, A. (2020, May 13).
What is gravity? livescience.com. https://www.livescience.com/37115-what-is-gravity.html

"Scientists have also proven a third theory that makes time-travel possible when combined with the <u>theory of special relativity</u> and the theory of general relativity[3]. And that is the <u>theory of relational relativity</u>, which determines whether an object moves forward or back as it relates to the direction the Earth moves on its axis. If an object moves in the same direction as the Earth moves, the object will move forward in time. If it moves in the opposite direction, it will move backward in time. A fourth is <u>the theory of time relativity</u>, which determines the time it takes to arrive at a destination.

Thus, our formula: Speed + Gravity + Direction + Time = Time/Space Travel

"Precise calibrations on the Transporter will determine the direction an object will travel, past or future, the bending of space time to determine the path it needs to take to get there, and speed. Since the surface of the earth at the equator moves at a speed of 460 meters per second. Or roughly 1,000 miles per hour in a 24-hour period, increasing the speed will project matter forward in time; decreasing the speed will project it back in time."

"I assume this theory has been tested?" Dr. Kannak asked.

"Oh, indeed," Dr. Emmit answered. "For purposes of testing and verification only, I, myself, have traveled both into the future and into the past."

----

[3] Tillman, N. T., Dutfield, S., & Bartels, M. (2024c, October 29). *What is the theory of general relativity? Understanding Einstein's space-time revolution.* Space.com. https://www.space.com/17661-theory-general-relativity.html

"Did you experience any adverse physical or mental complications?"

"None. As a matter of fact, from the beginning of the time being transported to the end, I felt relaxed, almost to the point of being sedated. And I arrived fresh and alert upon the arrival of both destinations as well as the return. Although a little hungry, I might add."

"I'm aware that I am to be transported to June 1 in the year 1978," Dr. Kannak said. "However, when am I scheduled for departure?"

"The day after tomorrow at eight o'clock in the morning," was the reply.

Chapter 3
May 31, 2042

After a much-needed good night's sleep, Amaq awoke at 7 am, readied himself for the day, and was on his way to the cafeteria for breakfast when he was greeted by Amanda.

"Good morning, Amaq. Are you ready to begin our big adventure?"

Rather surprised at the use of the word "our" in her reference to his traveling into the future, Amaq questioned, "Our big adventure?"

"Of course," she replied, as they found a table and sat down. Then, realizing his surprise said, "Oh, I'm sorry Amaq, I thought you knew. But come to think about it, that part wasn't covered at the indoctrination meeting yesterday, was it? So, how would you know? Well yes. I will be going with you. You see, realizing that you may need the support of someone who is knowledgeable about the workings of the Transporter, plus a sort of bodyguard to assist you in the remote possibility of trouble, the team thought someone should accompany you. And since I have that knowledge as well as combat training, I qualified. So, I volunteered."

As they walked to the cafeteria line to get cups of coffee and order their breakfasts, Amaq said, again showing surprise, "Combat training? Since when do physicists require combat training?"

"Well, normally they don't. But the first assignment I had with the FBSR was in 2023, right after I had received my Doctorate. The location was Namhkan, Myanmar, near the border with Yunnan, China, where the construction of the hydroelectric Shweli Dam had been completed in 2009, a joint venture between China and Myanmar. But by 2022, demand for electricity had increased beyond the plant's maximum megawatt capacity, and they needed to somehow increase that capacity. And since Myanmar had allied with China in their war with Russia over the statehood of Mongolia, which had been militarily annexed by Russia, Namhkan was declared a war zone. My assignment, of course, was to help develop plans for the dam's increased megawatt capacity within a budget neither warring countries could afford. But being stationed in a war zone, I was required to have hand-to-hand combat training as well as small arms training."

"So... guess what... like it or not, I'm your new bodyguard as well as your insurance to navigate through any problems we might have with the Transporter."

"Well, I hadn't anticipated this, but I can't say I don't like it... because I do. Not so much that you're going to be my bodyguard, but that I'm not going to be doing this alone. And I'm especially pleased that it's going to be you who will be accompanying me."

After they ate their breakfast, Amanda said, "Your next step is to see the Transporter Room."

When they arrived at the Transporter room, what Amaq saw was beyond anything he had imagined. It was a huge forty-foot square cavernous room with a ceiling that had to be at least as high. The space actually occupied floors 11 B through 14 B. The floor, walls, and ceiling, and even the doors, all looked like a pale blue cement had been sprayed on. It was, in fact, a thickness of 12 inches of a very dense sprayed-on acoustical plastic-like foam, which sound-proofed the room. Computer stations occupied about a fourth of the room, each having its own function for the operation of the Transporter. At least sixteen people were manning the stations. It reminded Amaq of the operations room at NASA, only somewhat smaller.

What appeared to be just a big black metal box completely occupied the remaining space. It had an eight-foot square door with eight-foot square windows on each side, which Amaq learned were 14-inch-thick tempered glass. This big black box housed the Transporter.

Amanda led Amaq through the doorway to view the enormous machine that was situated in the center of the housing. There was a vertical wheel at least 30 feet in diameter and six feet wide. It reminded Amaq of a treadmill worked by an animal running endlessly on a tread on the perimeter of a wide wheel having a horizontal axis... like a Ferris wheel. Only at Braxton Research, they simply called it *the wheel.*

"That's exactly what it is," Amanda said. "It's a treadmill... a *BIG* treadmill. But instead of being propelled by an animal running on a tread, it itself is the powerhouse that propels an object into *Time/Space.* Inside the wheel is a large oblong capsule, into which objects to be propelled are placed. It's not attached, nor does it rest on the wheel's tread; it hovers inside the wheel just above the lowest curve of the tread, which I might add, is exactly at ground level of this facility, so that it's at ground level when it arrives at its destination."

Amanda continued, "As we discussed in our indoctrination meeting, in order for something to move through *time/space*, gravity will bend time relative to how fast an object moves, the direction it's going, and the time it will take to arrive at a destination. In the past, all attempts for time travel were abandoned because it was thought that an object had to travel faster than the speed of light, 186,282 miles per second. However, who wants to travel that far in a second? We have proven that, with all the other variables, a speed of 76 miles per second, or 4,560 miles per hour, will move an object.

"The problem then becomes, 'how can we build a track, or tread, long enough to accommodate a vehicle traveling that fast?' That's if we could build a vehicle that can even travel that fast. The answer was the treadmill. Rotation of the wheel can reach a speed of up to 6,000 miles per hour, and the length of the tread is limitless, as is the path of a circle. By using a vehicle that can travel either backwards or forward, depending on the direction of the rotation, and hovers in place over the tread, it can travel in *time/space* to any destination which is determined by the time and speed set to travel."

Leading Amaq to a small room that served as a restroom, shower room, and changing room, she explained, "Before we enter the Transporter Room, we need to change into these Time/Space suits, which let us move about in a non-gravitational field in the Transporter Room."

Seeing the puzzled look on Amaq's face, Amanda said, "Oh, I'm sorry, Amaq. Here I am expecting you to understand theories of physics and this whole *Time/Space Project,* while I have absolutely no clue about the theories of virology. Let me back up here and explain.

"Anti-gravity (also known as non-gravitational field) is a place free from gravitational forces, otherwise called G-forces, or even simply Gs, with 1G equaling the pull of Earth's gravity. When we're in the capsule, the wheel will be rotating at a speed of 6,000 miles per hour, a speed at which the wheel could only remain intact without breaking up unless it was in a non-gravitational field, which we accomplished with anti-gravity technology.

"At a speed of 6,000 miles per hour, the wheel will project us one year into the past *Time/Space* in one hour. And since we will be traveling back 64 years to 1978, we will be in the capsule for 64 hours, a little over 2 ½ days."

After suiting up, the two of them walked into an anti-gravity chamber that was connected to the Transporter, wherein 1G was exchanged for 0 G. Now in a non-gravitational field, the door to the Transporter Room was opened, and they entered.

In spite of the magnetized boots of his *Time/Space* suit that kept him grounded, the sensation of weightlessness immediately threw Amaq awkwardly off-balance, which reminded Amanda of someone's first attempt at ice skating. Lightheartedly laughing at him, she said, "I should have warned you that in a non-gravitational field we lose all sense of weight that gravity provides and we have to adjust to it...but usually slowly and not without warning. Sorry. But now that we're here, let's get into the capsule and take a quick test trip into the past just so you'll get the feel of it. Tomorrow morning, being the real thing, time doesn't permit us to have more than this one trial."

Inside the capsule, there were four "Captain Kirk Chairs" (a time-worn phrase dating all the way back to the television sci-fi series of Star Trek seventy-four years earlier), arranged two sets side-by-side, accommodating up to four passengers. And there were storage compartments for whatever might be needed for a *Time/Space* voyage. The only control they had was a hand-held device called the Control Tower Phone, or simply the CTP device, which is about the same size as a TV remote control device. With it they could communicate with the central control tower where everything else was coordinated. Then all they had to do was sit and wait for the control tower to activate the process.

After they both strapped themselves into their chairs, Amanda pressed a button on the CTP device and said, "Central Tower, this is Dr. Kane. All is ready for transport." She released the button, and a reply came from the control tower, "Ready. On our countdown, ten – nine – eight – seven – six – five – four – three - two – one – begin rotation."

At that, the wheel began to rotate and it rapidly increased its speed. The noise it made became louder and louder until it reached a speed of 5,500 miles per hour, and the noise would have deafened the capsule's passengers had they not had the *Time/Space* suits on. At this time, Amanda said to Amaq, "Since we're traveling only one day into the past, when the speed reaches 6,000 miles per hour, we will have reached our destination after only 365th of a complete rotation. Be ready."

Almost immediately, the noise and all movement ceased. "We're here," Amanda said. "Welcome to yesterday." They both unstrapped themselves from their chairs, exited the capsule, and entered the anti-gravity chamber, which of course became a gravity chamber as they prepared to exit into the Transporter Room. To Amaq, she said, "What you see are all these technicians making sure that everything is ready for tomorrow's *Time/Space* travel, the one you and I just made."

"I understand. It's still just so mind-boggling. So, the day that we're now standing in is the day I arrived here in Braxton... yesterday. I would guess, then, that as we speak, you and I are also having lunch in the cafeteria."

"You guessed right," Amanda replied. Would you like to go up and see us?"

"You bet I would," Amaq answered. "Will we be able to see us?"

"Yes, but we didn't. While we were eating lunch, I looked for us in the off chance we might cross paths. But, we didn't."

When they arrived in the cafeteria, Amaq looked across the room and saw himself and Amanda having lunch.

"This is just too much!" Amaq said. "No, I don't want them to see us. I think if I looked over here yesterday and saw you and me, I wouldn't have been ready for the shock."

"Well, that explains why I didn't see us. You didn't want me to," Amanda replied. "We'd better get back down to the Transporter Room and suit up for our return voyage back to tomorrow."

Reversing everything they had done earlier, they traveled forward into the future and arrived back into the day in which they had originally begun.

"Amanda, I have a few questions that have been on my mind," Amaq said as they got into the elevator to go up to the main level. "Wouldn't we be able to travel into the future to discover if our mission into the past was successful? And if it was, shouldn't there be in the CDC storage vaults a sample of the vaccine they used to end the 1948 pandemic, as well as the formula for the vaccine? And if so, why couldn't we just as easily transport that back to our laboratories?"

"Yes, no, and yes," Amanda replied. "Yes, we could travel into the future to discover if our mission was successful. And we did that. And we discovered that our mission was successful. Knowing that should be reassuring. And no, they didn't have a sample of the vaccine. As are many other vaccines, the Mercedes Vaccine, as they called it, became very valuable. And because it could never again be formulated naturally because of the extinction of Fusarium, it became even more valuable. So much so, that it mysteriously disappeared from the CDC's storage vault, and as far as we know, it has never been recovered. It's been suggested that a vial of the Mercedes Vaccine would be valued at one million dollars in today's currency. And yes, if it had been in the CDC vault, we could have just as easily transported it back to our laboratories. All of which brings us to where we are now, preparing to venture into the world of the mid-twentieth century.

Amaq and Amanda spent the rest of the day gathering the things they thought they would need for their voyage into the year 1978. Their adventure would begin at eight o'clock the next morning.

Chapter 4
June 3, 1978

Even though they had been in a state of suspended animation for 2 ½ days, when Amaq awoke, he was surprised that he was remarkably refreshed and not even hungry or thirsty as he thought he would be. He and Amanda had awakened just as the sound of the rotating wheel faded into nothingness and the entire building they had been in slowly just disappeared, as did the non-gravitational field they had been in. The capsule that they were in was still in the exact coordinates it was in at the beginning of their voyage, but hovered alone in a permafrost plain strewn with volcanic rock where the Braxton Research Laboratories was later built. It would hover there until its occupants notified the control tower of their readiness to return, whenever that might be.

When they exited the capsule and changed from their *Time/Space* suits into hiking clothes, Amanda viewed the landscape and said, "Well, it's no wonder that this is where Braxton chose to build their laboratories. They wanted isolation, and this sure fits that description."

"Yet, it's only about four and a half miles to the Mekoryuk Airport," Amaq added, "where I'm hoping to hire a private plane to fly us to Anchorage."

Amanda said, "Too bad the road's gone. That was the first thing they built before they even began construction on the laboratory. But of course, it's not here now. Since trudging over permafrost terrain is like walking on a sponge, I'm guessing it will take at least three hours, maybe more, to travel that distance. So, we probably should get our things together and start walking."

They had already taken their backpacks with them when they exited the capsule. The backpacks, which were packed with their few personal belongings and the supplies the team had gathered, would be the only baggage they carried. If they needed anything besides that, they would purchase it as needed. In the supplies they put together, the team had included 50–100-dollar bills in counterfeit money they used in the 1970s as well as counterfeit passports of the same time period and IDs documenting them as researchers at Beijerinck Institute of Medical Science.

....

After three or so hours of walking northeast on a difficult terrain, they came to a dirt road which they followed to the Mekoryuk airport, a state-owned public use airport that was located three miles southwest of the central business district of the Native Village of Mekoryuk, a distance they didn't necessarily want to add to their journey. They needed rest and nourishment, but their chances of finding a restaurant looked pretty slim.

The airport had no control tower or runway lights, just a single gravel runway. When Amaq arrived at that same airport in June 2042, the FBSR had long since built a control tower and added runway lights, adequate for the use of their private planes. Because of the permafrost, the gravel runway was nearly always frozen, so it was also adequate for their planes and needed minimum maintenance.

However, prior to FBSR's purchase of the land on which the Braxton Research Laboratories was built, the airport was used only by bush-pilots who would occasionally transport supplies for the village, and rarely transport someone to somewhere on the mainland. The runway was also adequate to accommodate a DC-3 cargo plane that could land and take off on short runways.

Amaq and Amanda were in luck. A DC-3 had just unloaded a cargo of supplies for the village and was preparing to take off to return to its home base at the Merrill Field Airport in Anchorage. Its ETA was seven o'clock that evening. Perfect!

After Amanda explained to the pilot that their journey had been somewhat taxing so far, and their destination was also Anchorage, she asked if they could purchase passage.

"Name's Yuamil," the pilot, said, "Thanks for offering, but up here we're accustomed to helping each other without expecting payment. Certainly, you're welcome as long as you're O.K. with strapping yourselves onto a pretty uncomfortable metal bench affixed to the interior fuselage."

Thankful for their good fortune, Amaq replied, "Thanks for your generosity. A metal bench doesn't sound that bad after the journey we've just made. We'll gladly make do."

"Oh, and if you're hungry," Yuamil said. "I have some extra sandwiches and some strong black coffee you're welcome to."

"Thanks again," Amaq said. "We'll take you up on that too." Soon after boarding, they were on their way to Anchorage.

As they expected, Yuamil's ETA was precise. At seven o'clock, they touched down at Merrill Field Airport, an Anchorage municipally owned airport and home base for the DC-3 cargo plane.

Yuamil suggested that their best bet for a hotel would be the Holiday Inn Express, just 1.6 miles from the Ted Stevens Anchorage International Airport and only six miles from their present location. Then, from a public pay phone, he called for a taxi, which arrived twelve minutes later. Amaq thanked Yuamil for his assistance and invited him and his wife to join them for dinner at the hotel's restaurant later that evening. Yuamil accepted the invitation, and he and his wife Jissika met Amaq and Amanda at 8:30 that evening. They had made friends on this, the first day of their mission; friends they knew they would probably never see again, but friends nevertheless.

....

June 4, 1978

The next morning after a complimentary breakfast, Amanda met with the hotel's concierge to make flight reservations to San Diego, while Amaq went to the nearest Wells Fargo Bank and exchanged two of the $100 bills for smaller denominations as he didn't want to call attention to the fact that they were carrying large amounts of money. Just being cautious.

The earliest flight to San Diego was scheduled for two o'clock the next day. So, the two scientists, feeling guilty about enjoying themselves during such an important mission, spent their free time visiting the Alaska Museum of Science and

Nature and the Native Heritage Center. To get a feel for local tradition, they had spicy links of reindeer sausage with sauteed mushrooms from a street food vendor. And for dinner, they again ordered local cuisine of monster king crab, flaky halibut, and Kachemak Bay oysters.

Chapter 5
June 5, 1978

The next afternoon, after boarding and locating their seats on the airplane, Amaq took the opportunity of the time they were in the air to explain the next step of his plan.

"Our next destination is Guadalupe Island, and I'm sure it's going to present us with some challenges we can't foresee," he began. "So, we need to prepare ourselves for the unexpected. But because the island is the most probable place to find Monterey pines, we need to go there regardless of any dangers we might encounter."

"So, what's so challenging about the island?" Amanda asked. "It surely can't be more challenging than Nunivak Island."

"Well, I've never been there, but I've done my homework. It's a small volcanic island off the coast of Mexico's Baja California Peninsula in the Oceania with a total area of 94 square miles and a population of about 200 inhabitants, give or take, and is one of the most challenging places on earth to reach. Two words describe it: harsh and desolate.

"It has a rugged landscape consisting of two ancient, overlapping shield volcanoes, the largest, Mount Augusta, rising to about 4,250 feet in the north and the smaller, El Picacho, about 3,200 feet in the south.

"The woodlands are mostly dense, impenetrable thickets of shrubs and/or evergreen trees in the higher regions on the northern part of the island.

"The coast generally consists of rocky bluffs with detached rocks. The southern part of the island is barren, but there are fertile plateaus and trees on Mount Augusta, the northernmost part of the island, where we'll find the Monterey pines.

"One aspect in our favor will be the weather. In the summer months, the temperature is 72-80 degrees except in the higher elevations, where temperatures can be ten degrees cooler.

"There's only one runway for small planes to use. It's called the Airport Isla Guadalupe, but it can barely qualify as an airport. The runway is only 3,900 feet long and not completely flat; there's no airport terminal or air traffic control. There's no hangar at the runway or anywhere to park a plane once it has landed. So, planes arrive without ground communication, and must leave as quickly as possible in case another plane wants to land.

"A westbound dirt road from the airport, actually more path than road, leads to Campo Oeste, the main settlement on the island. It's a small community of abalone and lobster fishermen. Generators provide electricity, and a desalination plant provides fresh water.

"There are no phones, televisions, or any other kinds of communication other than some radio stations."

"What's the plan for getting us there?" Amanda asked.

"Helicopter, hopefully," Amaq answered.

When they arrived at San Diego International Airport, they went immediately to an information desk and inquired about helicopter service to Guadalupe Island. Again, they were in luck; they were directed to a helicopter tours service just a short distance from the airport. They hailed a cab and went directly to the location they were given, both feeling like providence was working in their favor, and they might be able to make up some of the time they were forced to squander in Anchorage.

"Good afternoon," Amaq greeted a young woman standing behind a counter in the reception room of Baja Air Service. "I'm Dr. Kannak and this is Dr. Kane. We'd like to speak with someone about service to Guadalupe Island."

"Good afternoon and welcome to Baja Air Service," the receptionist replied. "It's nice to meet you. You're in luck. I'll put you in touch with Captain Luis Martinez who just happens to be in his office right now. He's usually somewhere up there," pointing skyward.

Upon entering Captain Martinez's office, Amaq's attention was immediately drawn to the framed photos on the wall. Captain Martinez had evidently flown helicopters in two of the U.S.'s most recent involvements in foreign wars. As a young man, he was pictured with fellow pilots in Korea. As an older man, he was pictured in Vietnam. And in another case hanging on the wall were his combat medals. Amaq already liked and admired the man.

After introductions, and all three parties agreed on being called by their first names, Amaq explained their request for helicopter air service to Guadalupe Island. "Our goal is to reach the higher regions on the northern part of the island to study the woodlands."

As a precaution, he didn't mention the Monterey pines, nor that they would be taking a sample of Fusarium from the trees. In all probability, it would be illegal to remove a sample from the island without permission, and they just didn't have the time for bureaucratic hassles.

"Who did you say you represented?" Luis asked.

"We're conducting a study for the Beijerinck Institute of Medical Science in Minneapolis, Minnesota." In a sense, Amaq lied because a study wasn't really being conducted in 1978. In another sense, however, it was being conducted only in 2024.

"Does this have anything to do with the rapid decline of the pine trees?" Luis asked.

"Yes, it has everything to do with that," Amaq replied truthfully.

"I'm quite familiar with the island," Luis said. "And I know for a fact that there's only one place I can land that will get you close to that region of the island. From there, however, you'll have a steep, perhaps dangerous uphill climb."

"Thanks for the warning, or, for that matter, any other advice that you'd like to give us. We know there will be challenges, but our mission being as vital as it is, we're determined to meet those challenges. Before we go, however, we need to get a few more supplies. Can you direct us to a sporting goods store?"

"That depends. What things are you looking for?"

"Basically, we're going to need camping supplies such as a small two-man tent, light sleeping bags, a small camp stove, lanterns, canteens, and some dehydrated food packs; nothing fancy. We plan on being there no more than a couple days."

With a smile, Luis said, "Look no further, mi amigo," We are an outfitter as well as an air transport service. Follow me."

Amaq and Amanda followed Luis to a back room that had everything they would need. "Just get what you need," Luis said. "You can rent it daily for as long as you wish without having to buy anything except the food."

"Well," Amanda said, "we were certainly steered in the right direction."

After packing the added supplies into their backpacks, Amaq told Luis, "What we would like for you to do is take us to that place on the island you mentioned and in 48 hours pick us up at the same place. Will you be able to do that?"

"Certainly," Luis said. "If it meets your schedule, we can lift off tomorrow morning after breakfast, and I'll have you there before lunch. OK?"

Amaq agreed.

Chapter 6
June 6, 1978

The helicopter ride was uneventful with perfect weather conditions. There was nothing spectacular to see —just the ocean. But that, in itself, was beautiful and mesmerizing.

In less than three hours, Guadalupe Island came into view. As they drew closer, the pictures of the island that Amaq had studied came into focus, revealing an even more rugged terrain than he'd expected. From his viewpoint, there seemed to be no shorelines onto which boats could land, just cliffs and mountain slopes zigzagging vertically down to the sea. From the air, it looked like an elongated, flat, rugged, barren, rock-strewn terrain anchored on each end by volcanic mountains, the one on the northern end being the largest.

Luis slowly veered the helicopter towards the northern tip of the island, where, when in view, he said, "See that small stretch of beach just south of the northernmost point of the island? Just beyond that shoreline is the Northeast Anchorage, where boats can safely anchor and their small boats can come ashore to one of the few beaches on the island. That beach is where we'll be landing."

Shortly thereafter, Amaq and Amanda disembarked the helicopter with their backpacks, now fully packed with the camping gear they added from the outfitter room.

"Because there's not a lot of daylight left," Luis said, "I suggest that you pitch camp here tonight. You don't want to scale that bluff in the dark. It's going to be hard enough in the daylight."

"Our thoughts exactly," Amanda replied.

"Is it safe enough here at high tide?" Amaq asked.

"Just barely," Luis answered. "If you make camp up next to the base of the cliff, you'll be okay. Where we stand right now, however, will be underwater."

"Well, okay," Amaq said, checking the time; it was 7:12 o'clock. "So far, so good. Luis, we want to thank you. You're definitely a welcome asset to this study, and I'm pretty sure your name and the name of your business will be included in the study transcript at Beijerinck Institute of Medical Science, he lied." Actually, he will be recognized as an asset at the Braxton Research Laboratories, but he couldn't divulge that to Luis.

"Have a safe flight back to San Diego. The plan is to meet back here the day after tomorrow for our return flight."

"Roger that," Luis said, shaking hands with both scientists. "Good luck to you both. And be safe. Barring any complications, I plan to be back here about five o'clock in the evening on the day after tomorrow. If for some reason that I can't make it, I'll come the next day that I can at the same time. There's no way for us to communicate, so we'll just have to leave it up to lady luck."

Luis climbed into the helicopter's cockpit, gave a salute, waved goodbye, and with a big smile said, "See ya when I see ya."

Chapter 7
June 7, 1978

Amanda awoke about two o'clock in the middle of the night. The temperature had not fallen much after sundown as they had expected, and it was still about eighty degrees Fahrenheit, much too hot for comfortable sleeping. When she opened the flap of their two-man tent, she was taken aback a bit when she saw that, with the high tide, the ocean had expanded beyond what it had been when they set up camp, when the distance to the water line had been about forty feet. It was now only three feet from invading their camp. Luis had indeed been right... again. So, her plan to cool off with a walk along the beach being undermined by natural forces; she had no choice but to lie down on top of her sleeping bag and try again to sleep, while all this time Amaq slept quietly and deeply on top of his sleeping bag.

Refreshed, energetic, and optimistically anxious to face the day, Amaq was the first to wake up. He decided to let Amanda sleep a bit longer while he dressed, then heated some water to make some instant coffee in a three-cup collapsible camping pot on a mini-one-burner propane stove. He then removed all his gear from the tent, nudged Amanda, who signaled with a low moan that she was awake, and he began packing his backpack.

He looked up at the cliff that rose above them, trying to calculate the best and safest way to climb to the fertile plateau at the top where the woodlands they were looking for were to be. Through his binoculars, he could see footholds that protruded from the face of the cliff that would give them a reasonably safe path to the top.

"Good morning," Amanda greeted Amaq as she exited the tent. "Is that hot water I see?" While spooning her instant coffee grains into a plastic cup of hot water, she asked, "What's for breakfast?"

While they breakfasted on instant oatmeal, canned peach halves, and hardtack biscuits, Amaq explained to Amanda, "As best I could, I've made a map of the footholds that we should probably take to scale the cliff." Pointing to the lowest foothold, and then to the place on his homemade map, he continued. "It looks like this is the only reasonable place to begin our ascent. Because our backpacks will be a detriment to our climbing, we'll tie them together and pull them up with a rope when we get to a recess in the cliff big enough to do so. We'll repeat this until we get to the top."

After final preparations were complete, Amaq began the climb. He quickly discovered that the footholds he had so carefully chosen were well worn from being used by others many times before. This made him a little bit more confident of a successful ascent without incident.

About a third of the way up, he came to a recess in the cliff that had enough room for the backpacks and a person to move around. He untied the rope he had tied around his waist, the other end of which was tied to the backpacks down below with Amanda.

He yelled down, "Okay, Amanda, I'm going to hoist the backpacks up. After I start pulling them up, you can begin your ascent, following the same route I just took.

She had carefully watched Amaq as he climbed and, using the same route, began her climb after he began hoisting up the backpacks. After Amaq had hoisted the backpacks up to the recess, he began climbing again.

It took them nearly three hours to repeat this process until they reached the plateau. Exhausted from the climb, they lay there on a flat rocky area just looking up at white, puffy clouds that had gathered for a beautiful summer day.

After rising from their rest, they viewed what lay ahead of them and Amaq was elated, but not surprised, that it was exactly as his research had described it: a dense forest of Monterey pine. He knew that they were standing on the rim of the volcano, but that the crater had filled in by small eruptions over the ages and the cypress of the chaparral eventually took seed and grew into a forest that was nearly untouched, not only because of the difficulty of removing it from its secluded location, but also because the Monterey pine is twisted, knotty and full of resin not suitable for lumber.

With feet spread and both arms raised to the air, as if in a victory stance, Amaq excitedly shouted to Amanda as if he wanted the whole island to hear, "We've arrived! And our search for Fusarium can begin."

After they set up camp, ate a quick lunch of ramen noodle soup, again with hardtack biscuits, Amaq entered the forest while Amanda rested in camp. He began inspecting the base area of each tree where Fusarium would normally be found. And after no longer than twenty minutes and only about nine meters into the forest, there at the base of one of the trees was a sizable growth of the precious fungal plant. Looking around from where he stood, he saw that several other trees were also hosting the plant.

Deciding to wait until just before leaving the island, Amaq didn't fill his specimen pouch with a sample. It wasn't going anywhere.

"Amanda, Amanda!" he excitedly shouted as he exited the forest. "I have found it... in abundance; we need to look no further; our search is over, almost before it began."

Chapter 8
June 7, 1978

After sharing a moment of jubilation over their good fortune, Amanda said, "It seems that our prayers are being answered and providence is still on our side. Mankind the world over is going to benefit from our find as soon as we can get it back to the Beijerinck Institute."

Amaq said, "Yes, and if everything goes according to plan, we should be back to Nunivak Island in less than a week. From there, I plan to send the sample to the Institute by jet courier. And I plan to finally visit my family in Utqiagvik before I return to my home in Minneapolis."

"Sounds like a plan," Amanda said.

After a camp dinner made of dehydrated fish, dehydrated figs, and again those delicious hardtack biscuits, Amanda said sarcastically, "Absolutely scrumptious. Do you care for more, or do you want one of these delicious chocolate energy bars?"

"I'll pass on the fish, but one of those bars might be good." While opening the wrapping to the bar, Amaq continued, "We have until about this time tomorrow when Luis is to meet us back down on the beach to fly us back to San Diego. In the meantime, with this extra time we now have on our hands, how about doing some exploring?"

"That sounds great," Amanda said. "We still have time before sundown. Why don't we begin with you showing me where you found the Fusarium?"

Shortly thereafter, they were in the thicket of Monterey pines where Amaq had found the fungal plants.

"See," Amaq said, "it's all over the place; just there for the taking. It's hard to believe that in just two short years, all of this will have died out from disease."

"I agree" Amanda said. "Do you think there's anything else here except the forest of trees?"

"I don't know. Maybe some rock formations, or even some evidence of some long-ago volcanic activity." Amaq replied.

They walked on into the thicket, trying to maintain a straight line to keep their bearings and not get lost. And sure enough, it wasn't long before they came to a clearing in the forest where rock formations of various sizes lay on the ground, blocking any plant growth.

"Wow, these are really interesting," Amanda said, referring to the rocks. "As a physicist, it excites my scientific mind to think that they were spewed up from deep in the earth centuries ago. And look over here. It looks like a fissure in the ground. Do you think it might be a volcanic shaft?"

"I suppose it could be," Amaq replied. "Or maybe it's just an opening to a cave. In any case, we won't know unless we squeeze through it and survey it from the inside. It looks dark in there. Did you by chance bring a lantern?"

"I did, but only because it's getting dark. I hadn't planned on spelunking. Shall we give it a try?"

"Sure, why not. But you go first."

He was going into the unknown. So to be safe, before entering the fissure Amaq tied the end of a rope around a tree, coiled it to be played out, and tied the other end around his waist. Because the fissure was so small, Amaq was only barely able to squeeze through. But when he got inside, the space opened up enough to crawl further.

He called out to Amanda, "I'm in, but my movement is limited to a tunnel-like crawl space; not enough room for both of us. I'm going to crawl just a bit further to find out if it gets any larger. If it does, I'll come back for you."

The further he went into the fissure, the wider it got, but also darker. And because of the darkness, he couldn't see ahead far enough to see what awaited him. All of a sudden, he was thrust forward, and holding the lantern tightly, he tumbled downward through the tunnel about 20 feet on what he guessed was about a 15-degree incline. When he held the lantern up to survey where he'd been deposited from the tunnel, he found himself lying on his backside looking up at a ceiling about seven feet above him in a cavern like space of about twenty feet wide, lined with walls of a thick, black, glistening coat, evidently from a lava flow from the last eruption, whenever that was, that had forced a passage through a chimney and out the fissure in which he had entered.

Thankful that he had tied the rope around his waist, he climbed his way back up through the tunnel-like crawl space and back to the fissure where he'd entered.

"Well," he said to Amanda, "that crawl space ends in a cave-like space, which I think must have resulted from the volcano's last eruption. I didn't take the time to look around.

But it's safe enough and not too deep, and I thought that you might want to go back in with me to explore it together."

"You bet I would. It sounds exciting."

"You're not claustrophobic, are you?" He asked.

"Just a little," she answered. "But if I get that way, it sounds like it's not too far to retrace my steps and exit without experiencing serious effects. So... I'm game. Let's go. We only have about an hour left before sundown."

Amanda followed Amaq, and they were soon standing together in the cavern-like space.

"Unbelievable," said Amanda. "I never would have guessed that this was down here. And look, did you notice that opening at the far end of the wall? I wonder if that leads anywhere."

They both walked over to the opening and held the lantern up so they were able to see that, indeed, it did lead somewhere. But the light from the lantern wasn't bright enough to see far enough inside for them to make any assumptions about where that might be.

"It's too late in the day for us to go any further today," Amaq said. "Let's plan to come back tomorrow morning before we have to climb down to meet Luis, and see what we find."

With that, they both retreated back to where they'd entered and shortly thereafter, retired for the night.

Chapter 9
June 8, 1978

The next morning, they woke up early, feeling anxious to resume their adventure of exploring what they were now calling the cave. A short time after a repeat of the same breakfast they had the day before, they broke camp and secured everything in their backpacks so that everything would be ready by four o'clock to descend the cliff and meet Luis at five o'clock. They took with them a second lantern, a camera, some dried fish and fruit, two energy bars, more hardtack biscuits, and canteens of water. Planning to collect the specimen of Fusarium when they returned from exploring the cave, Amaq also took a spade and his specimen pouch.

There was not much to explore inside the cave. Every surface of the walls, floor, and ceiling was that thick, black, glistening surface they had seen the day before, apparent evidence of a lava flow from the last eruption, and nothing more.

Amanda suggested, "Now that we both have a lantern, why don't we see where that opening in the wall leads to, if anywhere?"

The opening of the tunnel was big enough that, if slightly stooped, they could walk in it. Because of the absolute darkness and quietness, orientation was difficult, and it was hard to tell if the floor they were on was flat, ascending, or descending. But it felt to both of them as if they were descending deeper into the tunnel. The tunnel was also getting larger; large enough to stand erect with room to spare.

"Look at the floor," Amanda said. It's suddenly become a fine, almost sandy soil. And look at the walls, they've become almost like sandstone, like soil that has been compressed for untold ages. That means that we've descended into an age when this part of the island was probably above sea level. And look...there are distinct impressions of Lycopodites on the walls, vascular plants that are spore bearing plants like ferns."

"What does all this mean?" Amaq asked, not necessarily of Amanda, but of a natural inquisitiveness. "Does it mean that the island sank below sea level, or that the sea level rose over the island?"

"I'm not a geologist," Amanda replied. "But I do have some knowledge about the formation of the Earth. The last ice age ended about 10,000 years ago. Sea levels rose rapidly, and the continents were formed to their present-day outline. Which means that this island was probably a part of mainland Mexico many centuries ago before it was separated by the rising sea."

She began taking photos of everything she thought was significant. She set the camera on a ledge, set the camera to a timed shutter, and posed with Amaq with the cavern in the background. She didn't know what would come of it, but at least she had evidence of the existence of the underground cavern and of their presence there.

In their search for a passage to go further underground, they discovered that, except for a fissure far too small for them to fit through, they could go no further. But in his search, Amaq spied in what appeared to be a hollowed-out space almost hidden by the shadows. As he looked further, he saw a skeleton of human bones.

"Amanda, come quick," he said excitedly. "Look, these are human bones. It looks like he might have been buried here in this space that may have been dug out by human hands. If he was, that might indicate that he was among the first hominids to bury their dead... Neanderthals."

With further examination, Amaq continued, "Also, the large size of the skull with its long, low brain case, and the mid-facial protrusions, further indicate that this is a skeleton of a Neanderthal going back at least 30,000 years ago during the last ice age. If I recall rightly, Neanderthals were usually found in Europe, the Middle East, and Asia. So, our discovery here might indicate that, somehow, there was a Neanderthal migration that extended to the Americas. Such a discovery would change the entire study of ancient man."

Amanda lost no time in setting the camera up and taking several pictures of the skeleton.

Looking at her watch, Amanda said, "As much as I'd like to take time to explore more, we just can't. If we're going to meet Luis as agreed, we need to go now."

....

When they got to the opening to exit "the cave", they were startled to see that while they were underground, a violent storm had blown in from the West. The heavy rain was driven almost horizontally by a strong wind, and the thunder and lightning were continuous while a vast bank of frightening heavy, dark clouds roiled turbulently in the sky.

In spite of being frightened by the awesomeness of nature, Amaq knew that he needed to brave the storm and retrace his steps to the campsite to see if the backpacks were still intact or if they had been taken by the storm. Against an overwhelming deluge of rain being slammed against him as he struggled to keep his footing, he finally found both backpacks blown by the wind a few feet from where they'd been left. He grabbed them by their straps and pulled them behind him as he reentered the forest.

"We're going to have to stay inside the cave until this blows over," Amaq said to Amanda, who, fearful for his safety, had been waiting for him to return.

"Oh, thank God you're okay," she said. "I was so afraid for you. I see that you were able to rescue our backpacks. Without them, we'd be pretty much out of luck."

"Speaking of luck," he said. "I'm quite concerned about Luis. I hope he had enough warning about this storm to postpone his flight. I hope he didn't leave San Diego and get caught in the storm. If he did, he would face a pretty uncertain fate. In any case, I'm sure he won't be landing at our rendezvous today. We'll check it out after the storm abates. In the meantime, tonight we'll play caveman... and woman. And if we're lucky, we might be able to have some supplies left for dinner, including soggy hardtack biscuits."

Chapter 10
June 8, 1978

At the Hungry Horse Diner, where Luis regularly went to lunch, he was finishing his second cup of coffee after enjoying "Today's Lunch Special," when he looked out the window that was next to the booth that he was sitting in, looked up at the sky, and said to himself, "It looks like the weather is going to be perfect for the rest of the day."

He left the diner, mounted his motorcycle, and rode back to work at Baja Air Service.

"Good afternoon, Jan," he said to the receptionist/secretary as he entered the building.

He'd already flown two sightseeing tours that morning, and the ground crew, which consisted only of Max, was getting the helicopter ready for another one scheduled for one o'clock. He'd be back on the ground in plenty of time for Max to get the helicopter gassed up and ready for his trip to Guadalupe Island.

"What's this afternoon's weather look like?" he asked Jan, whose computer was always interfaced with a weather map provided by NOVA National Weather Service.

"It looks pretty good," she answered. "There's a nasty front moving in from the West, but it's going to affect air traffic North of here. We should be okay. But we'll keep an eye on it."

At 4 o'clock, he checked the weather again, and it was pretty much the same. No red flags. Giving himself plenty of time to get to the island by five o'clock, he took off at three-thirty.

The weather front had remained stationary in its projection until it moved out to sea. Then the air currents, which are many times unpredictable, especially in the Pacific, pushed the storm in a southward direction, while at the same time increasing the velocity of the storm. Viewing the weather map, Jan became worried. It looked like the storm and Luis could intersect at Guadalupe Island at about the same time.

"Luis, Luis, this is Baja Air, do you read me?" Jan repeated several times in her attempt to warn him. But there was no answer. Atmospheric interference from the storm must have already disrupted transmission. Luis was on his own. Jan would pray.

The island was in view in front of him, and he could see the approaching dark clouds of the storm further to his right and thought there was a good chance he could outrun it and land the helicopter before it reached him. As he felt the excitement of hope swell within him, he loudly exclaimed, as if he was talking to the helicopter, "It's gonna be close, but we're gonna make it, baby!" He reached for his Saint Christopher medal he had hanging over the instrument panel, kissed it, and prayed, "Stay with us, God. We're almost there."

Suddenly, an inversion of air current that preceded the storm tossed the helicopter erratically in the air like a toy. Luis lost all control of the aircraft as it spun recklessly and plunged into the sea about a hundred feet from the shore.

In spite of being disoriented from being tossed around inside the helicopter before it went down, and being jarred with the impact of the helicopter crashing into the water, Luis still had the presence of mind, or perhaps just survival instinct, to unbuckle his safety belt and free himself from the helicopter before it began sinking into the deep waters.

He found himself still being tossed around, this time by crushing waves, however. The storm had arrived with a fury, pouring torrents of rain driven by fierce winds that swirled the waters of the ocean into ten-foot foaming swells.

Luis was submerged several times by the pounding waves, and had it not been for the life vest he always wore when flying above any body of water, he wouldn't have surfaced at all. He was hit from behind by what must have been a floating object from the helicopter. He reached around to grab hold of whatever it was and found that it was the floatable seat cushion from the cockpit. As he held tightly to the cushion, a silent prayer of thanks flashed through his mind before he lost consciousness.

When he woke up, he didn't know how long he'd been lying on the beach, not too far from where Amaq and Amanda had pitched their tent just two days ago. It was high tide, so he knew the sunrise was approaching. Acknowledging that, he also realized that he had to have been lying unconscious on the beach all night. He took inventory of his body to find out if anything had been broken. It had. His movement was interrupted by a tooth-achy pain in his ribs. When he tried to prop himself up, his left wrist folded under in excruciating pain. And the swelling on the back of his head hurt when he touched it. "Okay," he thought to himself. "So, I have broken ribs; I don't know how many. I have either a broken wrist or a badly sprained one. And I have a goose egg on my head; hopefully not a concussion. And lots of bruises, I think. Could've been worse, a lot worse. Thank you for staying with me, God."

With a great deal of painful effort, he stood, almost collapsed, then straightened back up. He looked for the wreckage of the helicopter, but it wasn't anywhere in view... nothing. It must have been washed further out to sea with the high tide, where it sank into the depths of the ocean.

Then, almost in a panic, he realized that he was alone with nothing except the rain-soaked clothes on his back and the life vest, beaten up pretty badly, no food or water, and no wreckage for rescuers to find. "Hang in there with me, God; we're not out of this yet."

Chapter 11
June 9, 1978

Amaq and Amanda both slept fitfully on the hard lava floor of the cave. They didn't need their sleeping bags to keep warm; it was a perfect 68 degrees F in the cave. But had their sleeping bags not been rain-soaked, they could have used them to cushion the hard floor. They awoke still groggy with sore muscles.

Going over to the entrance of the cave, Amanda was happy to see a glorious day outside. The storm clouds were gone, and the sun was shining through white, puffy clouds of a quiet summer day. They took their backpacks out in the open air and laid everything in them on the surrounding rocks to be dried by the warm rays of the sun.

Sorting through the food supply, Amanda recovered almost everything since most of the food had been stored in plastic zip-lock bags. They had little water left in their canteens, but rainwater had collected in the pockets of some of the rocks. So before using any of their own water to prepare breakfast, she went about filling zip-lock bags with water collected from the pockets.

When they finished their breakfasts of instant oatmeal, dried figs, powdered orange juice, coffee, and, of course, the hardtack biscuits that had also been saved. However, after eating breakfast, nine biscuits and instant coffee were all they had left of their food supply.

Not knowing, of course, that Luis had crashed the helicopter yesterday, and thinking ahead to leaving the island later on that day, Amaq said, "It's pretty certain that Luis wasn't able to meet us at the rendezvous yesterday. But I'm hoping that he'll be there today. Why don't we walk back to the top of the cliff to see if the storm caused any damage that might prevent us from descending the cliff? Then, after our supplies have dried, we can repack our backpacks and carry them to the edge, ready to descend when the helicopter arrives."

They had some difficulty getting through the forest of trees since the storm had strewn the forest floor with broken tree limbs and tangled bushes.

"The storm must have been stronger than I thought," Amaq said. "Without the shelter of the cave last night, we would've been more miserable than we were. I guess we should be thankful for that hard floor. At least it was quiet and dry."

When they got to the edge of the cliff, they looked, and from what they could see, the footholds were still damp and probably slippery. But they would be dry later in the day.

"Hey, wait a minute," Amanda said. "I think I saw something move down there. I did... look... somebody's down there." In an attempt to get his attention, she waved her arms and shouted, "Hellooo down there. Can you hear me?"

Whoever it was looked up and waved back.

"My God, Amaq, it's Luis."

"No, it can't be," Amaq said as he looked down and saw a man waving. "If it's Luis, where's the helicopter?"

"Is that you, Luis?" Amanda yelled down.

"Amanda. Is that you?" Luis yelled back. "Is Amaq with you?"

Amaq peered over the ledge of the cliff and shouted, "I'm here, Luis. Hang on, we'll be down as quickly as we can."

Amaq went back to the clearing where the supplies had been laid out to dry. He got the rope that had aided them in their ascent up the cliff and took it back to where Amanda waited.

"Because you're lighter and I might be a bit stronger, it might be a good idea if you went down to help Luis. He may be injured and need some help."

Amanda agreed.

"Here, I'll tie this rope around my waist as a precaution in case I lose my footing, and you play it out as I climb down. When I get down there, I'll tie it around Luis's waist and help him climb up if he needs it. I'll be the judge of whether we need to climb up individually or together. Either way, do your best to pull on the rope to give us added support while we're climbing. Sound good?"

"Sounds good," Amaq agreed as she began tying the rope around her waist.

Because the slopes were still a little slippery, Amanda lost her footing three times during her descent. Had Amaq not been on the other end of the rope she had tied around her waist, she would have tumbled to the bottom, and in all probability, to great harm, or even death.

When she got to the bottom, she could see that Luis was suffering from some injuries, including shock and a possibility of a concussion.

"Luis, I'm so glad that you're here and that you're safe. How did you get here?" she asked. "Where's the helicopter? When did you get here?" She had so many questions.

Since his ribs were in so much pain, even when he exerted himself with talking, Luis explained as briefly as he could.

"Good weather report went bad. Couldn't turn back. Crash landed. Helicopter swept out sea. Ribs, wrist and head injuries. Could've been worse."

"If I tie this rope around your waist so Amaq can help hoist you up, do you think you can climb up the footholds that I just came down on?"

"I'll try, but because I can't use my left hand, I'll need a boost from you on the other end. But we don't have much choice. We have to try. There's not much hope of being rescued here. And we certainly can't survive down here. If there is any hope at all, we have to climb to the top."

After Amanda untied the rope from her waist and securely tied it around Luis, he began his one-handed, painful ascent with Amanda hauling on the rope from above and Amanda pushing up from below him. It was agonizingly slow going, and each time they came to a recess in the cliff, they rested to re-energize.

When they finally reached the top, the two scientists helped support Luis as they made their way through the forest back to their campsite, where Luis collapsed from pain and complete loss of energy. Amaq and Amanda both worried about his well-being.

There were now three, one nearly immobile. What were they going to do? How were they going to survive? How would they be rescued? All of these things preyed on their minds as the day passed into evening.

Chapter 12
June 10, 1978

"How are you feeling this morning?" Amanda asked Luis. She had risen early, not of necessity, but because her mind was fixed on their predicament, and she couldn't sleep. She heated some water for instant coffee.

"Better," Luis replied. "It's amazing what a good night's rest can do for the body... and soul." Then, sarcastically, "But I'll let you know for sure after I get up off my stone mattress. And sure, I'd love a cup of coffee."

Attempting to add a little levity to her remarks to both Amaq and Luis, she said, "Give me a minute. Because that's all the time it's going to take to prepare breakfast. This morning's special is one hardtack biscuit each and a cup of coffee. And because of the demand for such a satisfying dining experience, the menu for lunch and dinner will be the same."

"I can't wait," Amaq said.

But Luis, who didn't know yet of their dire circumstances, said, "You're kidding."

"Nope," Amanda said. "I'm not kidding. Luckily, we have plenty of water, but after we eat our last hardtack biscuit, we're completely out of food. After all, we purposely packed light and planned to be here just a couple of days. Best laid plans..."

While they ate their biscuits, they began exchanging ideas on what they should do to alleviate their situation.

Amanda opened the conversation. Directing her question to Luis, she asked, "What chance do you think we have of being rescued?"

He replied, "Yesterday morning, before you discovered me, I saw two U.S. Coast Guard Search and Rescue helicopters do a slow fly-over over my Point of Destination (P.O.D). Since I hadn't returned to base in San Diego, coupled with the track of the storm that Jan was monitoring, and knowing my POD, she undoubtedly notified NOAA, who, in turn, notified the Coast Guard. But since my helicopter had been washed out to sea after the crash, they were unable to locate any wreckage. So, I'm probably assumed lost at sea... or dead. I doubt if any future rescue attempts will be made."

Amaq also questioned Luis. "If I recall, the ocean just beyond the beach is an anchorage where boats can safely anchor; is that right?"

"Yep, that's right. But rarely does anybody use that area to anchor their boats to come ashore, unless they're looking for a secluded place to sunbathe on the beach. As you know, there's really nothing else to come ashore for unless you want to scale the cliff like you and Amanda did. It may be days, maybe even weeks, before a boat anchors there."

"Well, if we can't hope to be rescued by air or sea, that leaves land," Amanda said. And that's not likely since nobody even knows we're here and we have no way to communicate."

Amaq offered his observation. "It looks more and more like we're going to have to walk out of here on our own."

"Looks like," Luis said. "But that's doable. It's not like we're lost a long distance away from civilization. The length of the island, from north to south, is only about 22 miles. And it's only about 6 miles at its widest point."

"Have you ever traversed the island on foot?" Amanda asked.

"Oh no," Luis answered. "I've only flown over it. I even landed on the airstrip once to pick up a package that I delivered to an address in Ensenada, Mexico. What I remember about that is that there are several dirt roads on the island. The main road goes along the top plateau, and other minor roads branch off to the towns. The main road intersection is at Campo Pista, where three roads intersect at the southwest end of the runway. One of the roads leads to Mount Augusta, where we are now. So, all we need to do is locate that road, follow it to Campo Pista, where, if we're in luck, there will be an airplane taking off or landing. Or, sometimes there's a car or truck waiting for an airplane to land carrying supplies for Camp Oeste, or "West Camp," a coastal town of about 200 inhabitants where we can probably hire a fishing boat to take us to Ensenada, Mexico, an eighteen-hour voyage. Or, if we're real lucky, there might be a boat that has a radio that can communicate with the mainland. If that's the case, we'll be able to have Jan send another helicopter to rescue us."

"How far would you estimate it is to Camp Pista?" "

"Oh, probably only about six or eight miles south of here as the crow flies. But because we'll be following a path that zigzags downward, it will reduce the stress of a steep downward climb. However, it also adds about three miles to the trek.

Right now, we're at the top of a 4,400-foot-high mountain, and Campo Pista is on fairly level terrain at about 250 feet above sea level. So, we'll be descending a little over 4,000 feet in, say, eight miles, or 500 feet for every mile. And because of my inability to move very quickly, it could take us a whole day, or even more, just to get that far. And that's if we don't encounter any unforeseen mishaps."

"You mean that if we left now, we might be able to get there by nightfall?"

"Probably. But honestly, I think I need to rest the rest of today and maybe heal some. But the two of you can spend the day looking for that dirt road and getting some rest yourselves. The next couple days might be pretty physically demanding, especially with no food to energize us. We can leave first thing in the morning.

Chapter 13
June 11, 1978

Early the next morning, Amaq went back into the forest and, with his hand-held spade, loosened a goodly amount of Fusarium from one of the trees and secured it in the specimen pouch. He then joined his companions, who were now ready to begin their trek to Campo Pista.

Amaq and Amanda carried all of the remaining supplies in their backpacks, relieving Luis of any burden at all that might further hinder his progress. With blue jeans, hiking boots, and jacketed hikers' vests, the two were also appropriately dressed for the trek. Luis, however, hadn't thought that piloting the helicopter for about four hours in the summer heat required more than shorts, a t-shirt, and sandals.

So equipped, they walked down the dirt road they had found the previous day.

The path had a slight decline as they walked, and Amanda said, "Well, this isn't so bad. We're even going downhill. At this rate, it shouldn't take too long to get to Campo Pista."

Being in the mountainous, volcanic region of the island, however, the downward path began to wind through mountain passes and several miniature volcanoes.

"I see what you meant when you described the terrain," Amanda said to Luis. "This isn't a walk in the park after all. At this rate, I'll be surprised if we arrive at Camp Pista by the end of the day."

They had begun their trek in the pine woodlands and followed scattered trees and chaparral until the path crossed a gully and petered out in a shrubland. It was there that they met their first obstacle. At this juncture, the path they were following branched off in two directions: one directly downward into a gorge, and another veered off to the west, apparently to go around the gorge.

Looking down into the gorge, they observed that the thicket of prickly shrubs was so dense it would be almost impossible to navigate.

After some deliberation, Amaq asked the other two, "Do you think it's a good idea to try to push our way through that thicket? It looks to me like our legs would be torn up a bit, especially Luis whose legs are exposed." The other two expressed the same sentiment, and they agreed to take the path to the west.

They'd gone less than a mile when the gorge below flattened out to a wider terrain with more widely dispersed shrubs. The path they had taken now turned south again and led them through the shrubs that had become navigable.

Thankfully, the sun shone brightly, which gave them some idea of the direction in which they were traveling. Although their detour had taken them westward, Luis was reasonably sure that if they continued to follow the path in a southward direction they would eventually arrive at the airstrip at Campo Pista.

As they slowly trudged through the rugged terrain, they came upon a small creek, beside which the path now followed.

Seeing the creek reminded Luis of something he'd forgotten. He said, "I'm pretty sure that I remember that there's a small lake located near the runway. It's likely that this creek is one of its minor tributaries. If so, we're headed in the right direction."

They resumed their trek after filling their canteens with fresh water from the creek and resting a bit. It was now about four o'clock, and the heat from the afternoon sun made progress a bit more strenuous. They were thankful that they were able to quench their thirst with the fresh water from the creek, but they were all beginning to feel the discomfort brought on by hunger.

Another couple of hours brought them into view of the runway. And from that distance, they also heard the engine of a small plane. At that, in spite of their fatigue, they ran towards the runway, hands in the air, shouting to be noticed by the pilot of the approaching plane as it sped down the runway. Suddenly, their hopes were dashed when they saw the plane lift off into the air. It had been taking off, not landing as they had thought.

In resignation, the three of them watched as the plane ascended into the air. But they had completed the journey on which they had set out that morning. Their excitement and joy were mixed with pride that they had succeeded; their efforts had not been in vain.

Now seeing what they had all missed in their excitement, Amanda said, "Look, down there; a couple of guys walking from the runway towards the camp. It must be the passengers that the plane had flown in."

The two men walked in the direction of the lone, deserted building still standing near a small lake. Hurrying to catch up with them, Amaq, Amanda, and Luis saw them enter the building. They followed, but instead of startling the two men by rushing into the building, Amaq cautiously knocked on the door. He waited for an answer that didn't come. He knocked again and said loudly, "Helloooo, we're friendly folks here, meaning no harm. It might be to our mutual advantage if we met."

The door opened, and both men exited the building. It wasn't difficult to detect that they were suspicious of their intruders. "Whadda ya want?" the bigger man said in an unfriendly tone. He was about two inches taller than Amaq, but otherwise about the same athletic build, African American, mid-forties, with black bushy hair. The other man was about as tall as Luis, mid-thirties, had the appearance of being Mexican like Luis, wore glasses, and was balding.

"We don't want anything," Amaq answered. "That is, unless you have some extra food. We haven't eaten in a couple of days. Otherwise, we're survivors of a helicopter crash off of the Northeast Anchorage and are seeking refuge. We started walking early this morning and have come this far."

"Oh yeah, we heard about you," the Mexican said in a heavy Spanish/Mexican accent. "Before we left Ensenada, our pilot was told to keep an eye out for the wreckage of a helicopter and maybe its pilot. Which one of you is the pilot?"

"I am," Luis answered, extending his hand to shake hands. "The helicopter's been washed out to sea, but luckily, I survived. The other two here were my passengers and are scientists studying the ecology of the island. My name is Luis, this is Amanda, and Amaq. What can we call you?"

"My name's Scott," replied the big man. "And this here's Eduardo. I spose you're wonderin' bout our clothes. We just been released from the Ensenada State Prison and came here just to get away from everything for a while."

Eduardo said, "When I was a kid, there used to be a campground here where my family used to come to camp. This building used to be a kind of visitors' center. Sometimes somebody would bring cookies to share. I was kinda hopin' somebody might've done that, but it looks like nobody even comes here anymore."

Scott said, "You might as well come on in. We got some food, but not a lot. I guess we can spare some candy bars. I hear they're good for energy."

"Why, thank you, Scott," Amanda said. "We're truly thankful for your generosity. The only thing we have to share is fresh creek water, if you'd like some."

"No thanks," Scott said, "We have plenty of our own.

"By the way, what's in the pouch that you're carryin'?" he asked of Amaq.

There not being any need to lie about it, Amaq answered, "Oh, just a sample of some type of mushroom that we came here to study."

"Right," Scott said, indicating that he really didn't believe Amaq.

To Eduardo, he said softly, "There's gotta be somethin' important in that pouch. Look at the emblem on the pouch; looks like government to me; maybe somethin' valuable."

Feeling somewhat of a racial kinship with his fellow compatriot, Luis asked Eduardo, "I know it's none of my business amigo, but I'm curious. Why were you in prison?"

"That's OK," Eduardo answered. "I'm an accountant, and I got greedy. I was caught embezzling from my employer, for which I was sentenced to three years in prison."

"How about your amigo Scott?"

"You'll have to ask him yourself."

"How about it, Scott? Why did you serve time?"

"That's none of your bizzness," he replied, creating an awkward moment of silence.

Amanda broke the silence, "Okay, well… it looks like you guys are planning to camp out here for a while. Is it okay with you if we share this shelter with you tonight? We plan to be on our way at first light tomorrow."

"Where you guys headed? Scott asked.

"Instead of gambling on an airplane landing here anytime soon, and losing valuable time, we probably should push on to Campo Oeste."

"If you're wanting to leave the island, that would be my choice, Senor," Eduardo, who seemed to know his way around the island, said. "It's only about a half day's walk from here and a lot easier hike than the one you made today from Camp Bosque."

"There must be a road to follow," Amaq said, more as a question than a statement.

"Sure," Eduardo replied. "About eighteen meters (60 ft) just south of here, you'll find a westbound dirt road that goes there."

As an excuse for the three of them to talk among themselves out of earshot of Scott and Eduardo, Amaq said to his two companions, "Let's go check it out."

Once outside the building, Amaq said, "I have an uneasy feeling about those two. I don't think they've been paroled from prison at all. I think they're escapees. I mean, just look at their clothes. Authorities don't parole prisoners back into society in prison clothes, do they? Don't they give them civilian clothes?"

"I was thinking the same thing," Amanda said. "I feel pretty certain that you're right, and we might be placing ourselves in harm's way if we stay the night with them."

"On the other hand," Amaq said, "if we don't stay the night, it might arouse their suspicions and give them reason to believe that we'd report their location when we got to Camp Oeste. That could give them reason to hunt us down and silence us."

Amanda began first. "So, you're suggesting that we stay?"

Amaq responded, "It might be safer."

"What do you think, Luis?"

"I, too, think it might be safer."

"Then stay it is," Amaq said. "Oh, and look over there.

There's the westbound road. And it's really a road that vehicles can be driven on. If we start early enough tomorrow, we might get there in time for lunch. I'm sure we're all looking forward to that.

....

Before everyone settled down for the night, Amanda took the handgun from her backpack and hid it in her sleeping bag. "Just in case," she thought to herself.

Scott's snoring was as unpleasant as his general demeanor. In spite of that, however, everyone was so tired that it wasn't long before they were all asleep.

It wasn't a noise that awakened Amanda about two-thirty in the middle of the night; it was the silence. Scott was no longer snoring. She silently and cautiously turned to a position where she could see that he was bending over Amaq.

With gun in hand, she stood and said loudly enough to wake everyone else, "Hey... what do you think you're doing?"

Startled, Scott froze at first, then rose slowly and faced Amanda, some feet away. "I'm just releavin' the professor here of his pouch," Scott said. "Any objections?"

Pointing the gun at Scott, Amanda said, "You bet there is. Put that down where you found it."

"What'er ya gonna do if I don't, shoot me?"

"If I have to."

"Must be somethin' pretty important in this here pouch to kill for it."

"You have no idea," Amaq broke in. "Only it's worthless to you here. Unless it's put into the right hands for research, it's just a form of mushroom."

"So," Scott continued. "What would the 'right hands' pay for this?"

"Nothing," said Amaq. "If you take it, they'll just send me back for another sample."

"Yeh, if you're still alive," Scott said.

At that, Amanda hurled herself at Scott, ramming her shoulder into his midsection. He rebounded with a downward crushing blow to her back, which drove her to the floor, temporarily winding her, causing her to lose her grip on the gun. As he reached down to get the gun, Amanda put her combat training into action by scissoring her legs around his legs which brought him face down on the dirt floor. Once again, he rebounded, as did Amanda, and they stood face to face, Amanda in a combat stance.

"I've got this," she said to Amaq and Luis, who were both about to intervene.

Scott swung fiercely to punch her, but with an evasive maneuver, she easily escaped the blows, which further enraged him. He rushed her in an apparent effort to muscle her to the ground to gain the advantage. But as he was about to make contact with her, she reached in, grabbed his arm, and with a movement using his momentum, he was flung upward over her and landed with a thud on the floor in front of her, too immobile to resist further.

By this time, Luis had recovered the gun. Handing it to Amanda, she said, "You hang onto it. I can handle these thugs."

Showing his surprise at Amanda's command of the martial arts, Luis said, "I guess you can! I've never seen anything like that before. Where did you learn to fight like that?"

"It's a long story to be told later," Amanda answered. "In the meantime, what are we going to do with them?"

"Well, we can't let them go," Amaq replied. "Without a doubt, they'll try to keep us from arriving at Camp Oeste now. To be on the safe side, I think that we should tie them up, leave them here, and notify the authorities when we reach the settlement."

After some discussion, the three agreed with Amaq, and while Amanda held Scott at gunpoint, Amaq and Luis tied Scott's hands and feet securely while he was still somewhat groggy.

Then, Eduardo, who had remained quiet and unobtrusive throughout the whole sequence of events, pleaded with the three who now held him captive.

"You probably guessed from the beginning that Scott and I are escapees and are on the run. Scott's a mean and dangerous man. He was serving a life sentence for clubbing a man to death with a baseball bat... first-degree murder. He befriended me because, having been given a prison term for a non-violent crime and considered by the guards to be non-threatening, I was given access to most of the prison to distribute reading material, which was my job. As such, I was able to put together a plan for escape, which Scott got wind of. 'If you go, I go' he told me. So, I escaped, but with an unsavory man as it turned out."

Amaq said, "You had only three years to serve your sentence. Why was it so important that you needed to escape?" he asked.

"I would have served my term without objection. But the reason I committed my crime in the first place was because my daughter is terminally ill and will die without being given regular doses of very expensive medications. I simply needed the money to save my daughter's life."

"So, how are her medications being paid for while you're in prison?"

"I hid the stolen money in a numbered account that only a trusted friend has access to. And he sees to it that my wife gets money once a month to cover her living expenses and pay for the medications. I feared that, if my wife was given access to the account, she might be forced to give it to the authorities. As it is, she doesn't even know who my trusted friend is. He just makes sure she just gets the money every month."

"So, if your daughter is receiving her medications, why did you need to escape?"

"Because the funds will soon run out. When it does, I need to get her across the border to San Diego, where my sister is living and has agreed to take care of her and see that she gets her medications. To do that, I have to get her across the border illegally. And because there is so much corruption in illegal border crossing operations, I don't trust anyone else to do it for me."

"I see," said Amaq. "I wish we could help, but I'm afraid our mission has priority over anything else and, as much as we might want to, we can't allow ourselves to be sidetracked or distracted. I'm sorry we can't give you any details except to say that what we're doing has to do with an international crisis."

Upon hearing that, Luis said, "Really, how can the rapid decline of the pine trees on this island be an international crisis? I thought that your study was simply to determine why they were dying."

"Well, it's a bit more than that, Luis," Amaq explained. "But don't be alarmed. Whatever we find isn't going to affect the world now. It's vital information for the future."

Eduardo interrupted and brought the subject back to his own predicament. "But you can help me... if you really want to. All I need to do is get to San Diego. And from what you've said, that's your destination too. Could I possibly join up with you? And if anybody asks, could you lie a tiny bit and say I was your assistant... or something?

"We'll talk it over and give you our answer in the morning," Amanda said, "which by the way, isn't that far off. We all better get some sleep."

Chapter 14
June 13, 1978

The next morning, Amaq told Eduardo of their decision. "We've decided to not tie you up and leave you here with Scott for the authorities to apprehend. You may join us as far as Campo Oeste, but then you'll have to be on your own. There's no way any of us can be held for suspicion of aiding and abetting a wanted criminal. If it comes to that, we'll deny that we even know you. Time is too critical for us. I hope you understand."

"Oh, I do... I do," replied Eduardo. "Thank you, thank you, and my little girl thanks you. May God bless you, amigos."

Before beginning their trek, Eduardo opened his backpack and took out the food that he and Scott had brought with them. They all ate heartily before they began their trek.

....

Seeing a few shanty buildings just ahead, the four of them knew they were entering Camp Oeste, a small town of about 200 people who were mostly abalone and lobster fishermen. It's on the north side of West Anchorage Bay that provides protection from the strong winds and swells that whip the island. And because it is, by far, the largest community on the island that needs supplies from the mainland, and the bay offers safe anchorage, most boats, small ships, or seaplanes choose that location to land.

It was mid-day when they arrived, so there were only a scattered few people who had remained in town while the others were either fishing, caging lobsters, or entrapping Guadalupe fur seals which, the Island being their last refuge, had become a large population, their rare fur providing trade for goods from the mainland.

Since the people spoke Spanish, or at least their own dialect of it, Luis and Eduardo both could converse with them.

Seeing an elderly woman sitting on a bench in front of one of the buildings, Luis greeted her and said, "Buenos Tardes, Senora. We're travelers in need of transportation to the mainland. Can you help us?"

"Si Senor, maybe," she answered. "A boat brings supplies for Campamento Sur (South Encampment) almost every week."

"Campamento Sur?"

"Si, it's a weather station staffed by a detachment from the Mexican Ministry of the Navy. I don't know what they do there, and they never come to town, but their supply boat anchors at West Anchorage, and their shore boats come ashore here and deliver the supplies with a truck they keep here."

"When do you think they might make their next delivery?"

"Actually, they're overdue. They were here about nine or ten days ago, so they're due any day now."

Luis repeated to Amaq and Amanda what the woman had said.

Luis thanked the woman and offered her a small compensation, which she gratefully denied. "Thank you, but coin is of no use here," she said.

"Before we set up camp," Amaq said, "let's wait and see if, by chance, the supply boat will anchor today."

"I don't suppose that there's a cafe in town where we can sit and have a cup of coffee while we wait," Amanda said, more as a question than a statement.

Eduardo responded, "Are you kidding? Look around you. What you see is what you get. Within view there are about fifty shanty buildings, spread from one end of the settlement to the other, each one being home to one of the families inhabiting this community. There are no stores. No restaurants. Actually, you can't buy anything on the entire island. Anyone visiting the island is completely dependent on what they bring with them. That's one reason the island is so challenging to hard-core, survivalist campers."

After thinking about that for a moment, Amanda couldn't imagine a life where merchandise wasn't available to everyone; a world in which such conveniences weren't available, even for basic human needs.

"But, how are the families on the island able to subsist without access to... you know... things; things we rely on to sustain our way of life?" she asked.

"That's just the point," Eduardo explained. "People here don't sustain *your* way of life. They live primarily at a subsistence level as gatherers, hunters, and fishermen whose subsistence depends entirely upon the fruits of their labor, trading any excess abundance of what they have as payment for things they have beyond subsistence living, like water and electricity. So, you see, operating a proper store of any kind for any type of merchandise, would be impossible."

"Unbelievable," Amanda said, the only word that could express her thoughts.

"Well, at least we have our own food now," Amaq said. "How about some lunch while we wait?"

They were in luck. At mid-afternoon, the old woman Luis had talked to earlier walked up to them and addressed Luis, "Senior, the supply boat is coming and will soon be anchoring. A shore boat will be coming ashore shortly after."

"Gracias, senora," Luis replied. "You are very kind." Then, turning to the others, Luis said, "Let's go down and greet them when they come ashore."

Chapter 15
June 14, 1978

"Bueno Dias, Senior, I'm Luis Martinez," Luis greeted the first member of the crew of the supply boat who disembarked the shore boat when it landed.

"Bueno Dias, my name is Jose Manuel Perez, captain of the *Durango*, a supply boat of the Mexican Ministry of the Navy. How can I be of service?"

"I'm a helicopter pilot who survived a crash a few days ago near the Northeast Anchorage. I and my passengers have since found our way here in hopes of being rescued."

"You may certainly join us on our return voyage to Ensenada. But I must warn you, it's an 18-hour voyage in some pretty heavy seas. Might I suggest, instead, that you avail yourself to our ship-to-shore radio?"

"Will I be able to radio San Diego?"

"No, that's too great a distance. However, I can radio our base in Ensenada, and they have several methods of communication with San Diego."

"Great. I'm the owner of Baja Air Service in San Diego. If they were contacted of our location, they would immediately send another helicopter to rescue us in a matter of hours."

"After we unload this shipment of supplies, you may accompany us back to the boat and write your message. We'll send it immediately."

Later, on board the *Durango*, Luis wrote his message:

ALL IS WELL. LOCATION: CAMP OESTE ON WEST SIDE OF GUADALUPE ISLAND. SUGGEST HELICOPTER LANDING ON BEACH TO TRANSPORT 4 PASSENGERS. LUIS

After sending the message, the captain asked Luis if he'd like to join him as he opened a bottle of Corona beer. Even though Luis had been on the island for only seven days without even the slightest of comforts, he savored his bottle of beer as if it might be his last. What joy!

Before they had finished with their refreshment, a reply from Jan came over the radio:

HALLELUJAH AND ROGER THAT. COPTER AIRBORNE IN 15 MINUTES.

"Sounds like someone's pretty happy to hear from you," Captain Perez said. "We'd better get you back on shore so you'll be ready to greet your rescuers. My guess is you'll be home for dinner tonight."

About ninety minutes later, and knowing from what direction the helicopter would be coming, the four companions gathered on the beach, focused their eyes eastward over the island and waited for that speck to appear in the sky that would soon land to take them home. Eduardo was the first to see it, and he began jumping up and down, flapping his arms, and yelling, "Down here... we're down here," as if the pilot could see and hear him. As humorous as it was, it wasn't long before the helicopter was in full view, and everyone was doing jumping jacks and yelling, "Down here... we're down here."

When the helicopter finally landed, Jan, Max, and Luis's wife, María del Carmen, jumped out and ran to Luis. They had all feared the worst, and after five days of no reports of a sighting that gave hope of a possible rescue, he had been presumed dead. Witnessing the joyous reunion brought tears to Amanda's eyes and a lump to Amaq's throat. Eduardo looked on quietly and hopefully as he thought about his wife and daughter and how joyous their reunion would be... someday.

Neither the helicopter nor its pilot was from Baja Air Service, as Luis had expected. The identifying name on the side of the helicopter read: U.S. COAST GUARD SEARCH AND RESCUE. They had opted, rightly so, to fly a rescue helicopter with enough capacity to accommodate ten people, including the pilot. There were eight altogether.

High in spirit, they all boarded the helicopter for an uneventful flight on a beautiful summer day with white puffy clouds dotting a deep blue, peaceful sky.

During their two-and-a-half-hour flight to the U.S. Coast Guard Base in San Diego, there was plenty to talk about: the doomed flight that ended in the ocean; Luis's rescue by Amaq and Amanda; their perilous trek from Camp Bosque to Camp Pista airstrip; the incident with the escaped convicts, Scott and Eduardo and how Amanda overcame Scott; Eduardo's story; the trek from Camp Pista to Camp Oeste and the assistance they received from Jose Manuel Perez, Captain of the supply boat. To the loved ones who had met them, it seemed like a rescue story ready to be written and revealed to the world.

Much to the relief of Amaq and Amanda, not much was said about their mission other than they were scientists studying the rapid decline of the Monterey Pine trees on the island.

They were met at the air base by reporters and a few curious onlookers. A week later, and after an interview with Luis, the rescue story was told by a reporter for the San Diego Star Tribune and Luis was duly recognized for his bravery.

Eduardo? Well, he just disappeared unnoticed. The three companions wished him well.

Amaq and Amanda were invited to Luis and Maria's home to make arrangements for their flight back to Anchorage, Alaska, join them for a home-cooked meal, and stay the night.

After talking it over with Amanda, Amaq said to Luis, "You've done so much for me and Amanda this past week. Without you to lead us out of that terrible situation we found ourselves in, we'd still probably be wondering about and half-starved on Guadalupe Island. We owe you our deepest gratitude. And although you will never know it, you've played a vital role in the future of mankind. And I assure you, you will be credited for it. As for staying the night, nothing could be better. But, although our mission requires all expediency, we're going to stay another day in San Diego and would ask that you let us stay here just one more night."

Luis and Carmen were happy that they would be able to spend one more day and night with their friends and readily agreed.

Before retiring, Amaq made flight reservations for Anchorage, Alaska, on June 16th.

Chapter 16
June 15, 1978

After breakfast the next morning, Amaq and Amanda hailed a taxi with directions to take them to the nearest police station.

When they were finally interviewed by a police Lieutenant, Amaq told a short version of their story. "While on a scientific mission on Guadalupe Island, we had the unfortunate circumstance of meeting up with a man named Scott, who we learned was a convict that had escaped from prison in Ensenada, Mexico. With us was one of your local citizens, a man by the name of Luis Martinez, owner of the Baja Air Service here in San Diego. He was the helicopter pilot who crashed on the island a week ago. Yesterday, with his assistance, we were able to subdue the escapee, tie him up, and leave him in an abandoned building at the island's airstrip. I think we secured him tightly enough that he will still be there."

While Amaq was telling their story, the Lieutenant had an assistant verify the escape from the Ensenada prison.

With a report in front of him, the Lieutenant said, "According to this report that we just received from the Ensenada, your story about escaped prisoners checks out. But the report says there were two convicts, one named Scott Garcia and the other named Eduardo Sanchez. It reports that they escaped together. Did you, by chance, see another man that may have been Eduardo? Do you think he might also be on the island?"

As they had previously agreed to do, Amaq and Amanda both denied seeing another man on the island.

"We'll need you to stay while we file an official report," said the detective.

"That's impossible," Amanda said. "We have an important agenda to meet, and it's urgent that we leave now. You have our statement. Do with it as you will."

"But you can't just walk out of here," the detective objected.

"Watch us," Amaq said as they got up and walked out the door.

The next day, followed by an exclusive detailed story, the headlines in the San Diego Star Tribune read:

"Local man Luis Martinez Aids in the Capture of Escaped Convict"

Again, Luis had been duly recognized for his bravery.

After leaving the police station, the two scientists went to Ashland University of the Sciences and asked for the location of the anthropology department. When they arrived, they met with Dr. Anthony, a professor of anthropology. They told him about "the cave" they explored on Guadalupe Island and gave him precise directions to its location. They described how they entered the fissure and crawled through a tunnel-like passage that opened into a larger cavern-like space, then descended further into an age when that part of the island was probably below sea level at one time. They showed the pictures they'd taken of impressions of Lycopodites on the walls and told him of their theory that the island was probably a part of mainland Mexico many centuries ago before it was separated by a rising sea during the ice age. They also showed him pictures they had taken of the skeleton of human bones with its large size skull, its long, low braincase, and the mid-facial protrusions, indicating that it was a skeleton of a Neanderthal going back at least 30,000 years ago during the last ice age.

At the request of the professor, they remained in his office, answering questions till late in the afternoon. The professor had written five pages of notes before they left and vowed to organize an expedition to the island in the very near future.

Chapter 17
June 16, 1978

The flight from San Diego to the Ted Stevens International Airport in Anchorage was uneventful. Upon their arrival, Amaq and Amanda both were almost giddy with excitement. Just being back in Alaska lent to the excitement that they were only a day away from completing their mission.

They checked into the Holiday Inn Express, as they had only thirteen days previously at the beginning of their mission. "Oh yes," the reservation clerk said. "I see that you were here on June 3. Did you enjoy your visit?"

Without answering the clerk, Amaq and Amanda looked at each other, knowing exactly what each other was thinking. What they had experienced in the past couple of weeks could not, by any stretch of the imagination, be considered a "visit." It had been an adventure that neither one had anticipated. And to them, it seemed impossible that they had been in that exact same place in the Holiday Inn Express just thirteen days ago. It was as though it had been far longer than that. They just knowingly smiled at each other and, in unison, simply said to the clerk, "Yes, thank you."

After getting settled into his room, Amaq put a call in for Yuamil, the bush pilot who had given them passage in a DC3 from the Mekoryuk airport at the beginning of their mission.

"Hello, Yuamil, this is Doctor Amaq Kannak..."

"Amaq, my friend," Yuamil broke in. "How are you and Amanda? After you explained your mission to me and my wife, Jissika, at dinner a couple weeks ago, we've wondered if you'd completed your mission yet and if it was successful."

"Long story," Amaq said. "But we're going to be here overnight again, and if you and Jissika would like to join us for dinner again, we'll tell you all about it."

"We'd love to," Yuamil replied. "Same time, same restaurant, same hotel?"

"Yep, the same. In the meantime, we're in need of a flight back to the Mekoryuk Airport on Nunivak Island and were hoping we could rely on you to either fly us there yourself or assist us in finding another source."

"Of course. I'll do some checking around, and we can talk about it tonight."

That night, at dinner with their friends, Amaq and Amanda enjoyed their first full-course dinner since they had returned: King Crab and Kachemak Oysters with a glass of crisp sauvignon blanc wine. After the customary polite dinner conversation, they told their captivated guests about their experiences on Guadalupe Island.

"That's quite a story, or should I say adventure," Jissika said. "Do you think you'll be going back to follow up on your findings in "the cave"?

"Probably not," Amanda answered. "Or at least not for a while. Right now, there are more pressing matters that we need to focus on."

"I'm still not sure why it's so urgent to discover the cause for the decline of the Monterey pine. Is it in danger of extinction? And if it is, why is that so important?" Yuamil asked.

It wasn't Yuamil's intention to put Amaq on the spot. But, in fact, being unable to tell the whole truth about their mission, Amaq knew he'd boxed himself in. He had to improvise.

"Well, yes, the Monterey pine is in danger of extinction," Amaq truthfully answered. "But the importance of its extinction is not the loss of the trees themselves, but the extinction of what's causing its demise, and that's a fungal plant pathogen named Fusarium circinatum, which will become extinct with the extinction of the trees. And Fusarium is used in the formulation of one of our most vital, lifesaving medicines," not mentioning that that medicine was a future vaccine. "We need to study it so, hopefully, we can artificially duplicate it," he lied. "And that's why we needed the sample I've brought back."

Amanda looked at Amaq with an obvious look of amazement that Amaq had contrived what was a believable answer, yet so factually twisted at the same time.

"I see," Yuamil said. "I wish the scientists well at the Beijerinck Institute of Medical Science. But I thought you said that was in Minneapolis. Why do you have to go to Nunivak Island?"

"Oh Boy, here we go," Amaq thought to himself.

Surrendering to the fact that he now had no other choice but to lay it all out to Yuamil and Jissika, he began, "Look,

Yuamil, I'm going to tell you something you won't believe. Amanda and I are from the future, the year 2042, to be precise. I'm a microbiologist at the Beijerinck Institute in Minneapolis, Minnesota, working with a team of scientists to develop a vaccine to inhibit the spread of a virus that is decimating our world population at a rapid rate: a recurrence of the same virus that we had in 1948 called the Mercedes Virus. We have, in fact, developed that vaccine with the exception of one essential ingredient in the formula... Fusarium... which did, in fact, become extinct in 1980. And that's why I had to come back in time to gather a sample from which we'll be able to grow, in its natural state, quickly enough to inoculate everyone within a year. And Amanda is a physicist who works with a team that has developed time travel at Braxton Research Laboratories, a facility that was built in 2036 about four and a half miles from Mekoryuk Airport. In order to return to 2042 with my sample, we have to get to the exact location on Nunivak Island where our *Time/Space* capsule is."

"You can't have made that up," Yuamil said. "Yet, you can't expect a whole lot of people to believe you either. I'm convinced, but that's probably because, as a pilot, I've seen evidence of supernatural occurrences as well as what I think is an extra-terrestrial phenomenon. So, it's not that hard for me to imagine that a way to travel in time will be discovered in the near future. Wow, the more I think about it, the more excited I get. Jissika and I are the first ones on the planet to actually talk to a man and woman from the future."

"Well, not exactly," Amanda broke in. "We've talked to a lot of people in the last couple of weeks. But you two are the only people to whom we've told about our being from the future."

Jissika questioned, "I suppose this is all top secret, and we're going to have to swear not to divulge any of this."

"Not at all," Amaq answered. "You can tell whatever you like about us to whomever you like. However, like you yourself said, you can't expect a whole lot of people to believe you. And as of tomorrow, we won't even be here to verify what you might divulge."

"Speaking of tomorrow," Yuamil said. "I'd like to see with my own eyes the *Time/Space* capsule you talked about. You say it's just been sitting there, out there in the open?"

"Yep, only it's more like it's hovering."

"What's to keep someone from breaking into it or even stealing it?"

"For one thing, it appears to be seamless with no access. Only Amanda can open the hatch. For another, it's made of a new alloy that would withstand any assault, even explosives. And lastly, no force can move it from its location. It's in a fixed position that's programmed from Braxton in 2042. It's immovable."

"This I gotta see," Yuamil said. "I tell you what. I'd like to make a deal with you. I don't just fly DC3s. I also have access to a four-passenger helicopter, which I'm pretty sure will be available tomorrow. If you know the coordinates of where the capsule is, I'd like to bypass the airport and fly you directly there so we, Jissika and I, can be there when you two enter the capsule and disappear into the future."

Amanda replied, "Sounds like a win-win situation to me. What do you think, Amaq?"

"I couldn't have imagined a more perfect scenario," Amaq answered.

To Yuamil, he said, "Nothing could be better. Honestly, I think providence put you on our path to help us succeed in our mission. And you and Jissika will be welcomed as members of the project when I file my report. What you're going to do tomorrow will go down in history in 2042. How about that?"

"Oh, I can't wait... I can't wait," Yuamil said excitedly. Rising from his chair at the table, he said, "Let's get back to the house so I can make arrangements to use the helicopter tomorrow. I think there's still time to call my friend Nanurluk, who owns the helicopter."

Then he added, "I just can't wait. Hurry up, let's go!"

Chapter 18
June 17, 1978

With permission from Nanurluk to use his helicopter, the party of four arrived at the Merrill Field Airport just after eight o'clock the next morning. Nanurluk had arrived an hour earlier to make sure that the helicopter was fueled and otherwise checked out for flight. At his suggestion, they all walked over to the small airport cafe for a light breakfast. For many years, he and his wife had been friends with Yuamil and Jissika, and before they took off, he wanted to enjoy their company as well as meet the two scientists he'd been told about.

They chatted like old friends do. Then, addressing Amaq and Amanda, Nanurluk said, "Yuamil tells me that you two are scientists studying what's causing the decline of a pine tree native to Guadalupe Island."

"Yes, that's true," Amaq replied. "And for most people, that's pretty boring. What's not boring, however, is what our names tell us about each other. My full name is Amaqjuaq Kannak, one that you undoubtedly recognize as an Inuit name... as is yours. My guess is that your hometown is in the North Slope Borough as is mine. My hometown is Utqiagvik."

"I thought I recognized a brother beneath that academic exterior," Nanurluk said. "And you're right. My hometown is Atqasuk, less than a day's travel from Utqiagvik by dogsled. We have a lot of things in common, brother that most folks know nothing about. How in the world did you get tied into science? And how long has it been since you visited your family in Utqiagvik?"

"The answer to your first question… long story. Suffice to say, however, that it was my choice, and I worked hard to get my doctorate.

"The answer to your second question is… too long. Within the next few days, my hope is to visit my family. I miss them. Sometimes, I even miss the Inuit way of life. It'll be refreshing to set foot on Inuit ground again.

"And yes, we do have a lot of things in common. What's your family's last name? Whenever I do get to visit, I'll make it a point to look up some of your family," not mentioning that that would be in 2042.

"My full name is Nanurluk Anawak. And my family is well known in the small community, as is everybody's. Just mention my name, or your own Inuit name for that matter, and you will be welcomed by everybody."

"Well, if Jissika and I are going to get back here by mid-day," Yuamil said, "we'd better get the helicopter loaded and get ready for take-off."

All five boarded the helicopter and were soon flying west towards Nunivak Island.

....

Three men left the *Blue Loon Cafe* in Mekoryuk, donned their helmets, and mounted their dirt bikes for a riding adventure over the island's tundra landscape. They were all family men and hardworking walrus hunters; the walrus being what the Nunivak peoples depend on to survive, holding much of the necessities of living in the Bering Sea area. But today, they were going to leave it all behind them and enjoy the beauty of their island and its challenges.

About seven miles out, one of the bikers stopped his bike, and as the others pulled up beside him, he pointed to a shiny oblong thing ahead of him and said, "What's that up ahead? I've never seen anything like it before. Let's go take a closer look."

They suspiciously approached the object, which made no motion.

"Where do you suppose it came from?"

"I have no idea. And look, it doesn't even touch the ground. It's just sitting there in mid-air like it's hovering."

"Hush, listen. Do you hear that low humming sound?"

"Must be a battery or something inside holding it in suspension."

"Let's get closer and see if we can open it."

"Where's the opening? There aren't even any seams. If there were seams, I could try to pry it open with my pocket knife. But it's completely smooth... no possible way to open it."

"Guys, do you know what we're looking at here? I think it's from outer space."

He took out his pocket knife and tried to scratch the surface, but no matter how hard he tried, it didn't leave a mark.

"See," he said. "It isn't made of anything we have on earth. I bet if we tried to blow it up, we still couldn't damage it or even move it. It's spooky."

"Listen, what's that?"

They all looked up in the sky and saw, as well as heard, an approaching helicopter.

....

Closing in on the coordinates he was given, Yuamil told his passengers, "We're nearing our P.O.D. (point of destination) and should be touching down in about five minutes. As they got closer, he pointed downward and asked Amaq, "Is that what we're looking for?"

"It sure looks like it... yep, that's it... that's the capsule." Amaq confirmed. "And it looks like it has some company."

Yuamil held the helicopter in a holding position over the capsule as the passengers watched three men below scramble like they'd been caught doing something wrong. They all three mounted their dirt bikes and sped away before Yuamil landed the helicopter.

"I wonder how many people have stumbled across the capsule like those three bikers did," Amaq said.

"Way out here, probably not many," Amanda said. "But it really wouldn't matter. It's indestructible, immovable, and impenetrable. And I'm the only one here who can open it."

Yuamil landed the aircraft, and they all disembarked.

"Unbelievable," Yuamil said as he and Jissika slowly walked around the capsule in awe of the object in front of them.

"How do you get inside," Jissika said. "There's no door. It's smooth, just like an egg... no cracks or seams. And what's keeping it from falling to the ground? It's just hanging there, suspended in mid-air."

"I can't answer all your questions," Amanda said. "Just suffice to say it's twenty-first-century physics."

"We probably wouldn't understand anyway," Yuamil said. "Can we take pictures?"

"Sure, all you want," Amaq answered.

After taking several pictures of the capsule from many different angles, Jissika asked, "How about some pictures of our space travelers."

"Why not?" Amaq answered. "Nothing here is secret. And I guess if there's any proof that we've been here, taking pictures is probably the best thing you can do."

The two scientists posed for several pictures of themselves in front of the capsule.

Then, with her camera and with Jissika's camera, Amanda took several pictures of Yuamil and Jissika posing with both, the helicopter and the capsule in the background.

Amanda said, "These pictures will be worth the proverbial thousand words when we submit our report. And I'm sure one or two will be framed and hung on my office wall as a reminder of our twentieth-century friends.

Then Jissika set up the camera tripod, and pictures were taken of all four of them standing in front of the capsule.

"Well, I guess it's time to prepare for our journey," Amaq said. And with that, Amanda placed her thumbprint on the very top of the capsule. Suddenly, as if magically, a square made of thin-line cracks appeared on the side surface of the capsule.

"Is that the door?" Yuamil asked. "Where's the handle?"

To answer the question, Amanda placed her index fingerprint in the middle of the square, and it swung open, exposing the inside of the capsule. Their friends looked on in total amazement.

Amanda reached inside the capsule and removed their *Time/Space* suits. After changing into them, Jissika asked if they could take more pictures. "Nobody's going to believe this," she said. "They're going to believe this is just a movie set or something. Maybe if I get pictures of all four of us in front of the capsule, it will remove the Hollywood impression."

With both scientists suited up for their *Time/Space* voyage, Amaq said, "Well, it's time to say goodbye. It's not to say that we won't ever come back... because we can. But the only way you can visit us is to grow forty-six years older. And when and if you do, look us up. You're the only ones who know about the virus that's coming. I wish you could change the future by warning everyone, and even persuade health officials to stockpile for future use some of the serum they used to eradicate the virus in 1948. But it would be a futile attempt. You can't change the future... or the past, for that matter. But, at least you two can keep yourselves safe and live well. Perhaps we'll meet again."

Amanda reached back into the capsule and retrieved the two syringes already filled with the proper amount of serum to keep them in suspended animation for their return trip. They injected each other, then entered the capsule, secured the door, and strapped themselves in their Captain Kirk chairs.

"Control tower, this is Dr. Kane. All is ready for transport," Amanda said into the CPT device. And they were off, leaving their friends looking at an open, empty landscape.

From behind some rocks, the three bikers watched the whole thing, and when the capsule disappeared with the two suited scientists inside, one of them said, "Yep, gotta be aliens from outer space."

Chapter 19
June 20, 2042

Still feeling extremely groggy from having been in a deep sleep for 2½ days, Amaq turned over onto his side to resume sleeping. Before getting too comfortable, however, he opened his eyes, looked around, and realized that he was in a hospital bed and an IV had been put into his left forearm. "What th...."

His thought was interrupted by Amanda's familiar voice, "Hello, sleepy head, we thought you were never going to wake up."

Amanda's face came into focus and Amaq said, "Amanda... where are we?"

"We're back at Braxton Labs," she replied. "We've only been back for about ten hours, but you didn't recover from the suspended animation serum as soon as they had expected, so they put you here in the infirmary for observation just to be on the safe side."

Slowly getting his bearings and putting things into perspective, Amaq said, "Then everything's okay? We successfully completed our mission?"

"Yes, Amaq. We completed our mission, and the sample of Fusarium circinatum that we brought back with us is already on its way to Beijerinck Institute by special jet courier. By this time tomorrow, it should have been planted and growing, duplicating itself at a rapid rate. The first batch of vaccine should be available for inoculation in about two weeks. And even though our mission took longer than anyone anticipated, they're finally going to have the capabilities to irradiate this terrible virus."

"Hey, guess what," Amanda said, pointing to the television. "We're on TV."

She had already had the pictures developed that had been taken by Jissika before they entered the capsule for their return trip to 2041. The reporter who had been commissioned to cover the story immediately emailed the pictures, along with what he knew of the story so far, to the television station ALNN (Alaska News Network), which was now being broadcast.

Two scientists, Dr. Amaqjuaq Kannak and Dr. Amanda Kane, returned from the year 1978 by way of the Time/Space-Project at Braxton Research Laboratory in Alaska. They successfully located and retrieved a sample of a fungal plant pathogen that was available in 1978 but became extinct in the early 1980s. With this pathogen, scientists will now be able to complete the formula for a vaccine that will be used to eradicate the Mercedes virus.

"The country is cheering your success," Dr. Kenneth Willard said as he entered the room. "Congratulations. You're both heroes and have become household names. If this was another time, you'd be whisked off, making millions to make appearances and speeches. As it is, however, your work is in more demand than ever. Especially you Amaq."

As a nurse was removing the IV in his arm, Amaq said, "I know, no rest for the wicked, as they say. But they can carry on without me at Beijerinck Institute. All the research and trials have been made already and they have the knowledge to get the Fusarium planted and growing without me. There are two weeks before it can be introduced to the present formula and testing can resume. And I'd like... no... I insist that being this close to my hometown, I'm going visit my family before returning to Minneapolis."

"Understood," replied Dr. Willard. "If I was you, I'd do the same thing. Also, I'm sure that you don't need anyone's permission to do so. The entire nation is in your debt, and nobody would deny you of that."

"I don't understand why my work is in demand more than ever, either," Amanda said. "You got along without me for a couple of weeks, and you can get along without me for another couple of weeks. Besides that, I have about six weeks of vacation built up. I want to go with Amaq if he'll have me."

"If I'll have you?" Amaq blurted out. "You've become as much a part of me as my right arm. Of course, I'll have you. To be honest, I don't know what I'd do without you."

"You really know how to make a girl feel special, don't you?" Amanda said. "Besides that, the feeling's mutual. After the last two weeks, it's going to be real hard getting back to work without you. We do make a pretty good team, don't we?"

Getting out of the ridiculous hospital gown they had him in and putting on his street clothes, he said to Amanda, "I'm starved. How about you? Meet me in the cafeteria in a half hour, and we'll make our plans. Next stop... Utqiagvik."

Amaq was the first to arrive in the cafeteria and, by chance, picked up a copy of the June 18 edition of the Anchorage Daily News(paper). He was immediately shocked when he read the latest casualty statistics resulting from the Mercedes Virus. Out of a world population of 8.6 billion people, 4 billion, nearly half, had contracted the virus; 1.98 billion had died, 23% of the world population. Out of an estimated 400 million population in the United States, 175 million had contracted the virus, and 8.4 million, 21%, had died.

Another article reported that the Beijerinck Institute of Medical Science predicted that by the end of the month, their scientist will have a vaccine to eradicate the Mercedes virus within a year.

Amanda joined him at the table, and he handed her the newspaper, saying, "In our two-week absence, another million or so people have died of the virus. Being delayed, as we were, cost the lives of more than a million people.

"Have you called home yet?" Amanda asked.

"No, not yet. I haven't even unpacked my backpack yet, and I don't even know where my cell phone is," Amaq answered.

"Not to worry," Amanda said. "I unpacked your backpack for you, and I have your cell phone right here. It might be a good idea to call home to see how the virus has affected that region of the globe."

Amaq replied, "Good idea. I see that you're still taking care of me. Thanks."

When he called home, Amaq's mother answered the phone. After telling her he was coming to visit, he asked her how the virus had affected the people in the North Slope Borough.

"No sickness here," she said. "Something about being north of the Arctic Circle."

Chapter 20
June 21, 2042

Amaq's mother, Ahnah, hung up the phone and excitedly called to her husband, "Nukilik, that was Amaqjuaq on the phone."

Walking into the kitchen where Ahnah was, hand cupped to his ear, Nukilik asked, "What's that, you say?"

"I just talked to Amaqjuaq," she answered. "He's going to be here tomorrow. Says his plane should be landing at the airport about noon."

"Who?"

"Amaqjuaq. He's going to be here tomorrow.

"Well, why didn't you say so? How long's it been since he's been home? Couple years?"

"More like three or four," she corrected him. "He came home for the entire summer before he went to that school in Minneapolis to get his Doctorate. We hear from him now and then, but he hasn't been back here since."

"He didn't give us much notice," Nukilik said. "We're going to have to clear out all that stuff we've been storing in his room before he gets here."

"I don't think so. He said that a woman was with him, and they plan to stay at the Tukkumavic Suites Hotel, you know, the one down on Ahkovac Street; it's not too far away."

"A woman, huh? You think he might have gotten married?"

"He didn't say, just that a woman was coming with him."

"And they're both staying at the hotel... together?"

"Well, he didn't say they'd be sharing the same room. But if they do, he's not our little boy anymore, you know."

"We're going to have to get a hold of his sister and brother," Nukilik said. "They'll probably want to go with us to greet them at the airport."

Chapter 21
June 22, 2042

Having made arrangements for Amaq and Amanda to be flown to Utqiagvik by the corporate multi-engine airplane, Dr. Kenneth Willard drove both scientists to the Mekoryuk Airport early the next morning.

A little before noon, the pilot announced to its two passengers that they were approaching their destination on schedule and would be landing in about three minutes.

Looking down through a cloudless sky, Amanda was surprised to see a town that appeared not to be unlike any other small town in the northern climes. Since Amaq had always referred to his hometown as "the settlement," she had imagined just that... an Eskimo settlement.

As they touched down on the single asphalt runway and taxied to the main hub, she noticed that it was a small but modern airport with what appeared to be a base for at least eight aircraft: one jet, three helicopters, one multi-engine airplane, and three single-engine. As they got closer, she saw a sign that read:

WILEY POST-WILL ROGERS INTERNATIONAL AIRPORT

Two things caught her attention. "Why would they name the airport after a famous aviator and an American humorist?" So, she asked Amaq. "And I'm surprised that this is even an international airport."

"Well," he answered. "En route to Utqiagvik in 1935, Will Rogers and Wiley Post made an unplanned stop at Walakpa Bay, fifteen miles away. When they took off again, their plane stalled and plunged into a river, killing both of them. As a memorial, the airport was named after them.

"And as far as being an international airport, it's the only airport in the North Slope Borough that accommodates jet aircraft. And with over thirty landings per day from as many as fourteen nations, its designation is international."

After a perfectly executed three-point landing, Amaq and Amanda, luggage in hand, walked into the airport terminal and were immediately greeted at the door by Amaq's family.

"Welcome home, son." Along came hugs and kisses.

"Amaqjuaq, you old son-of-a-gun," came a voice, and there landed a brotherly slap on the back.

"Oh, I'm so glad to see you," said his sister, barely able to contain her sisterly love for him and gave him a kiss and hug.

It was now time to introduce new members of the family. "This is my wife, Adlartok and my son Tokla," said Amaq's brother.

"Oh, it's so good to see all of you," Amaq said. "Mom, Dad, I'd like you to meet Amanda, a fellow scientist with whom I've been working for the last three weeks. Amanda, my mom and dad, Ahnah, and Nukilik.

"And, Amanda, I'd like you to meet my brother Inuksuk, his wife Adlartok, and their son Tokla... and my sister, Tanaraq.

By the way, Tanaraq, where's your husband, Kallik?"

"He was called to assist in Anchorage, where the virus is rampant. When he got his degree in medicine five years ago, neither one of us... or anybody else for that matter, could have imagined the horror that's been inflicted by this virus."

"Yes, and it's for that same reason that I've not been able to visit my hometown for so long. We've been working day and night, 24/7, to formulate a vaccine for the virus. But now we're this close to success, holding his thumb and forefinger about a quarter inch apart. And Amanda's been working with me.

"By the way, Mom, you said on the phone that there haven't been any cases of the virus here in Utqiagvik. Has anybody been able to account for that?"

"I think it's been hard enough to determine what causes the virus," she replied. "But the medical profession has pretty much figured that out. What they can't seem to figure out is why we, here in Utqiagvik, don't get sick. But we're told that, for some reason, cases above the Arctic Circle are zero. And we don't even use precautionary measures like face masks, social distancing, and testing. All they can conclude is that lower atmospheric temperatures protect us from being infected. But nothing conclusive; just a theory."

There was no way that Amaq and Amanda would be allowed to check into the hotel. Amaq's family had already made sleeping arrangements: Amaq and Amanda both could stay with Amaq's parents if they chose to share the same bed. If not, Amanda was welcome to stay with Amaq's sister, Tanaraq.

It wasn't the first time that Amanda's feelings for Amaq surfaced. Their experience on Guadalupe Island had occasioned them to sleep side-by-side many times. More than once, she had felt the warmth of his body next to hers... and she welcomed it. In spite of the temptation, however, she chose to stay with Tanaraq. She didn't know how Amaq felt, but at least her decision would dispel any thoughts his family might have had about the closeness of their relationship.

Leaving the airport, they all convened at Mom and Dad's, the home they all shared while Amaq was growing up. As with nearly all the houses in Utqiagvik, their home was a simple two-bedroom house with a third bedroom added on. Because of the permafrost, most homes were raised above ground with no basements.

Like the town itself, the home was in no way primitive, but it was basic. Like most communities in Alaska, Utqiagvik looks temporary, like a pioneer settlement. But it's not at all. Since the North Slope Borough was established in 1972, the borough has created sanitation facilities, water and electrical utilities, roads, fire departments, and health and educational services.

The south section of town, called the "Barrow side", serves as downtown, including the airport, an elementary school, Barrow High School, City Hall and police station, a Wells Fargo bank, hotels, and restaurants.

Mom and Dad's home was in the Central section called Bowraville. In addition to the houses in this residential area, it boasts of a library, a US Post Office, a Middle School, a hospital, two grocery stores, one hotel, two restaurants, and the Inupiat Heritage Center.

Chapter 22
June 23, 2042

"Good morning, Tanaraq," Amanda said as she walked into the kitchen where Amaq's sister was preparing breakfast. Is there something I can help you with?"

"And good morning to you," Tanaraq replied. "And yes, you can get a couple of plates out of the cupboard there. I'm just finishing up breakfast. I hope you like walrus. And because I know it's a favorite in the lower states, I brewed some coffee too."

"Walrus… for breakfast?" Amanda thought to herself. Looking at what Tanaraq was serving, she knew she was about to experience something new. "And, oh no, some hardtack biscuits too?"

"Did you sleep well?" Tanaraq asked as they sat down to eat.

"Oh, very, thank you," Amanda said. "Even though we're experiencing the midnight sun, I slept very well.

After sampling the meat, Amanda was pleasantly surprised. "This is quite good," she said. "I've never eaten walrus before and didn't know quite what to expect. Is this something you often have for breakfast?"

"Not too often, but it is one of our favorite foods." And she explained: "We rely mostly upon subsistence food sources. Whale, seal, polar bear, walrus, waterfowl, caribou, and fish are harvested from the coast or nearby rivers and lakes. And because they're available in the summer, we get to add some roots and berries, like what we're having with our breakfast… a real treat. Unlike you, however, plants are missing from our diet because they don't grow in these harsh conditions, and they're too expensive to import. We're pretty self-sufficient and don't rely too much on imports."

"I would guess, then, that fishing, whaling, and hunting are some of the main occupations here," Amanda said, more like a question.

"Oh, yes. And our natural resources not only provide us with our food, but they also provide the materials for our clothing, which we also make.

"We're also surrounded by the National Petroleum Reserve, which provides employment. And numerous businesses provide support services to the oil field operations, which adds to our economy."

While both of them were cleaning up after breakfast, Amanda said, "I understand there's an Inupiat Heritage Center here that has a pretty good library. Do you know if they have computers that the public can use?"

"You heard right, Tanaraq answered. "It's the Tuzzy Consortium Library that also functions as the academic library for Ilisagavik College. I go there often; I like to read, and it's my resource for books. But I've never had an occasion to use a computer. But my guess is that they have them."

"Well, I know that Amaq plans to spend time with his family, look up some old friends, and visit some of his old haunts. And while he's doing that, I think I'll visit the Heritage

Center to learn more about the culture here and look up something I've been wondering about."

. . . .

To enjoy the balmy forty-degree weather, Amanda walked the few blocks to the Heritage Center, a modern building that looked out of place on the unpaved street, as did the other buildings that she walked by. She understood, however, that the roads in Utqiagvik were unpaved due to the permafrost.

She was happy that the library did indeed have two public-use computers. She could spend the rest of the day, if need be, to follow up on something she had been wondering about. In her report of the *Time/Space* journey to 1978, she had recorded in great detail the visit she and Amaq had with Dr. Felix Anthony at Ashland University of the Sciences in San Diego about their discoveries in *the cave*. And she was curious if Dr. Anthony had organized an expedition to Guadalupe Island to explore their findings as he had vowed.

Accessing the Internet, she typed in Dr. Felix Anthony's name. Then, she again typed in the doctor's name on the Anthropology Journal website. She was astounded by what she found.

Felix Jerome Anthony; 1932-2017. Focusing on indigenous/prehistoric man in North America in his doctoral thesis, he received his doctorate in anthropology at the age of 24. After serving as a teaching professor for twelve years at the Ashland University of the Sciences in San Diego, California, he was appointed head of the Anthropology Department. During his tenure at Ashland University, he conducted "digs" each summer with selected students, resulting in a catalogue titled: **Discoveries of Prehistoric Man in North America.**

107

Fascinated, but impatient to find what she was looking for, Amanda fast-forwarded to a section titled:

Discoveries of Prehistoric Man on Guadalupe Island, Mexico.

Dr. Anthony's most recent contribution to the field of anthropology centers on a discovery made in the Guadalupe Island, Mexico. "Credit for the discovery should be recorded as having been made by two scientists who visited me in June of 1978, Dr. Amaqjuaq Kannak, a microbiologist specializing in virology, and Dr. Amanda Kane, a physicist with a background in quantum physics,"

Dr. Anthony explained in a recent interview. "Upon an exhausting investigation, however, nothing has ever been documented about either of them."

Following up on the report from the two visiting scientists, Dr. Anthony visited the island in the summer of 1979, where he, indeed, located the site on which the discovery had been reported. And in the summer of 1980, he organized an expedition to the site. The discoveries made on that historic expedition are now documented in the annals of science and credited to the discoveries of Dr. Felix J. Anthony.

The expedition team documented indisputable evidence that during the last ice age that ended about 10,000 years ago, sea levels rose rapidly, thus separating Guadalupe, by about 150 miles, from the west coast of Mexico's Baja California Peninsula in the Oceania.

Further discoveries revealed evidence that there was a Neanderthal migration to that area about 30,000 years ago, thus proving scientific theories of the existence of prehistoric man in North America.

Chapter 23
June 23, 2042

When Amanda finished her inquiries about Dr. Anthony and the discoveries he had made during his expedition to Guadalupe Island, she printed selected pages to show to Amaq when she would join him later that evening.

In the meantime, Amaq was enjoying visiting with his father as they walked through the town Amaq had been raised in. Although he'd been away from the traditional Inuit lifestyle of his youth for several years, it was so engrained in him that he felt like he'd never been separated from it.

They walked north by the elementary school Amaq had attended, the Barrow High School from which he graduated, and the City Hall and police station… all filling Amaq with happy, familiar memories.

They spent the better part of the day following Stevenson Street, stopping at familiar places along the way and reminiscing. All the while, Amaq had been noticing that the distance between the street and the ocean was narrowing. At one point, he stopped, and pointing towards the beach, he asked, "Dad, I'm sure I remember a hotel and restaurant right over there. They're gone. What happened?"

"You remember correctly, son," his father answered. "But that's not all that's gone. So are many of the old buildings that were used to process meat and hides. As you know, climate change and the warming of the Earth have caused the melting of the Arctic ice, swelling the Earth's oceans. Each year, our beach is getting narrower and narrower as the ocean creeps onto our land. And since the town is only ten feet above sea level at its highest point, the ocean is swallowing our land at a rapid rate each year. Since you were here last, we've lost fifteen feet of land mass."

When they walked further on, Amaq saw ahead of him where the street ended. Had the street continued on its past path, the Pacific Ocean would have been on the west side, and what was called Port Moore would have been on the east side. However, covering the land that then separated them, the two bodies of water were now joined and all points north of that were now under water as well as all of the off shore islands that were natural habitat for waterfowl.

Nukilik, Amaq's Father, had been the Shaman for the North Slope Borough for as long as Amaq could remember. As such, Amaq had always listened to his father's wisdom, not only because he was his father, but also because he was the community's spiritual advisor. Because he alone was chosen to mediate with the unseen world of gods, demons and ancestral spirits, he alone could receive and interpret their wisdom.

Shaken by the probability that his homeland may someday be completely overtaken by the rising ocean, just as the land that connected Guadalupe Island with the Mexican mainland had, Amaq sought his father's wisdom now. They retraced their steps until they found a bench in front of one of the remaining buildings. There they sat as Nukilik closed his eyes and began to speak.

"Many centuries ago, our people had their beginnings with the existence of unseen spirits separate from our bodies, but joined in nature. But we began to distance ourselves from those spirits, the spirits that gave us the wisdom to live peaceably with all of nature and with our fellow man. And that "distancing" is when our relationship with all of nature and our fellow man began to decline. As a result, we have suffered famine, wars, pestilence, disease, financial ruin, and natural disasters. We were warned by our ancestral spirits, but we didn't listen.

"But what can be done now?" Amaq asked. "Is it too late to make things right again? Or will we continue to suffer these things?"

"We have tried to overcome our suffering with knowledge and technology, forgetting to rely on the wisdom of the spirits. You, yourself, live in a world that is continually striving to create a better world… in a world that was already at peace, at one with nature, at one with his fellow man, and at one with the spirits of those who went before us.

"To overcome famine in the world, we grow more food, but fail to distribute it unselfishly as the spirits would have us do.

"We make treaties with neighboring countries, but fail to honor them.

"We build nations with mightier and more powerful resources, but fail to build stability that comes only through the spirits.

"We race to cure disease with chemicals and scientific medical advances, but fail to understand the nature of things… and the things of nature… that heal, as well as our relationship with the spirits that heal.

"We put our hope in financial resources only to realize, at some point, that what is built up is eventually broken down.

"And we try to counter natural disasters with hallow efforts to change nature.

"So, to answer your question, Amaq, the spirits tell me that our only hope is to return to our traditional religious practices in which good things manifest themselves through the unseen spirits and our union with nature."

Amaq sat silently for the wisdom of the Shaman, his father, to process in his mind. Then he said, "Surely, you're not saying that all human suffering can be overcome by returning to our traditional religious practices. Are you?"

"No, certainly not. Suffering is the nature of things on this earth. It's not our enemy. It's a natural thing. But we must meet our sufferings head-on while putting our hope in the wisdom of the spirits of those who went before us and in the things of nature that live with us."

"We didn't realize it at the time, but the task that Amanda and I just finished, was a race to the cure with a substance found in raw nature… one revealed to us through the spirits. I can also see where science, combined with nature and the spirits, can sometimes produce amazing results. We talked of providence many times during the last couple of weeks. And I believe that the spirits were with us."

"So, how are the people of Utgiagvik going to deal with the impending disaster of losing their homes to a rising sea?"

"Unlike the governments of the world that like to blame the excesses of man for climate change, and legislate to control man's actions related to it, we of nature's children know that what's happening is not unique; that climate change is an ongoing phenomenon that is not caused, nor controlled, by man. Our people, therefore, surrender to it. There is no other choice. Nature will always prevail.

"So, as our people have been forced to migrate before, we shall do so again. Many have already relocated to the cities and towns further inland. Many have stayed together and have begun small communities. Not much will change with us…only location."

....

When Amanda joined Amaq after dinner at Mom and Dad's, she and Amaq did some congratulatory back-slapping for the role they played in Dr. Anthony's expedition to "the cave" on Guadalupe Island.

Then, they stayed awake until the early morning hours discussing Nukilik's vision of… well, of… life. They concluded that one needn't choose between traditional Inuit spirituality or a Christian theology, or a balance of both – religious syncretism – it all resulted in the same thing… reliance on a power much greater than our own.

Before retiring and saying good night to Amanda, Amaq said, "Oh, I almost forgot. I want you to join me and my family in celebrating one of our local festivals over the next two days."

Chapter 24
June 24, 2042

The next morning, Amanda was awakened by someone gently nudging her. It was Tanaraq. "Wake up, Amanda, we're going to be late," she said. "We're expected to be at Mom and Dad's to help get ready for the Nalukatag."

"The what?"

"The Nalukatag."

"What's that?

"It's the spring whaling festival that we celebrate in the third week of June every year."

"That must be what Amaq was talking about last night; something about celebrating one of the local festivals the next couple of days."

"Actually, the next three or four days. And we're expected to help prepare the quaq and muktuk."

"Again, what's that?"

"Quaq is frozen whale meat and muktuk is whale blubber and skin. Nalukatag is the first of several times during the year when it's distributed to the community... a tradition of sharing.

"So, what do we need to do to prepare it?"

"Except for some that we prepare to be eaten at the festival, we take what we've put aside since our last sharing and divide it equally between communities. Everyone else does the same, and every community gets an equal amount. Sometimes we get less than we give, sometimes more. But we all get equal shares. Like I said, it's a tradition of sharing."

....

For the next three days, everyone from Utgiagvik and surrounding communities participated in and enjoyed the Nalukatag. Food was plenty and music was played by local musicians. There was dancing and singing. And groups gathered for storytelling. And Amaq was in the gayest mood Amanda had ever seen him in. It seemed he knew everybody, and everybody wanted to share his homecoming. And he wanted everybody to know Amanda as well, so, she was by his side throughout the festival.

On the second day, Amanda learned that the namesake of the festival was characterized by the dramatic Eskimo blanket toss. It was the focal point of the festival, where at least a hundred or more spectators formed a huge circle around those who held onto the edges of a huge blanket and tossed the contestants into the air as they tried not to fall and to reach the tallest height. It was dramatic and it was exciting as the crowd cheered them on.

On the third day, Amaq was urged by his friends to be a contestant. And although he wasn't tossed the highest, he at least didn't fall.

His friends then urged Amanda to follow suit. "Amanda, Amanda, Amanda," they shouted until she relented. It was great fun and exhilarating, but she fell on the twelfth toss as the crowd cheered.

115

The Nalukatag was the best thing that could have happened to Amaq and Amanda. For the first time working together side-by-side, they were able to put out of their minds all of the trials that they'd shared… all the frustrations of the obstacles that they'd had in their rush to quell the horrors of the virus. And now the pondering of the Shaman's visions of an uncertain future. Once again, they talked of providence and were thankful for the moment.

Chapter 25
June 27, 2042

Returning to Mom and Dad's after a brisk morning walk with Amaq, Amanda's satellite phone rang.

"Good morning, Amanda." She recognized the voice. It was Dr. Kenneth Willard, the Project Director at Braxton Laboratories. Knowing that he wouldn't have called unless it was about something urgent, she wished she hadn't even answered the phone.

"Good morning," Amanda answered.

"I'm sorry to bother you."

"If he only knew," she thought.

"But something's come up, and I'm afraid that I'm going to have to ask you to return to Braxton as soon as possible. It's urgent."

"It always is," she thought.

"I can get my things ready and meet the plane when it arrives at the airport," she said, not too happily. "Just have the pilot call me with an ETA."

"Thanks, Amanda. I knew I could count on you. Goodbye, I'll see you sometime tomorrow.

Amanda had enjoyed the last few days so much. It was disheartening that she was going to have to cut her vacation short. What she dreaded most was having to tell Amaq that their being together had come to an end. She would be going her way, and he would be going his. They had grown so close and shared so much in the past month that neither of them let themselves think of the inevitable, even though they both knew they would someday have to say goodbye. That someday was today.

But first, they were both dedicated scientists, and it didn't take long before that reality set in.

"What is it that's so urgent," Amaq asked.

"Dr. Willard didn't say," she answered. "But climatologists from around the world have been indicating for some time now that their sciences aren't such that they can predict very far into the future. As such, developing a plan of how to deal with our present climate change and the devastating results of global warming, is almost impossible. They claim, and subsequently have been very persuasive, that we need to see into the future to be able to make those plans. I have an idea that that's what's so urgent."

They stood together on the runway as the plane approached.

"We met on a runway," Amaq said as he and Amanda faced one another, both hands in hand. "And it looks like we'll be saying goodbye on another runway. Thanks, Amanda; we made a great team, and I'll miss you. Together, I think we made a difference, and I'll soon be going back to Minneapolis to finish our work."